THE FIDDLER
IN THE NIGHT

A NOVEL

Christian Fennell

Firenze Books

ACCLAIM FOR
Christian Fennell's
TORRENTS OF OUR TIME

"Whatever expectations one might have of a book of dark, realist short stories set in rural America, this collection defies them, and instead weaves an elegant song of sadness, dark humour, and strangeness."

~ *Neon Books, UK*

"Visceral and raw. Abstract and compelling. This book is simply Douglas Adams but written for small-town America. This is a Hitchhiker's Guide to small-town America."

~ *N. N. Light's Book Heaven*

"Many of Fennell's stories, which employ different narrative techniques, create effective tension and suspense."

~ *Kirkus Reviews*

"Christian Fennell writes stories to savour. Sharp, salty and sly, they come at you sideways with a shot of poignancy when you least expect it - and a twist of humour when you most need it."

~ Katy Darby, Director,
Liars' League London

"Beautifully moving and profound prose."

"With his transformative sentences, Fennell skillfully connects the reader to his protagonist."

"Words used to be art. In their creation. In the act. And thus the words were art in their very being. Forget the reader. Just don't forget the impetus. Christian Fennell never did. One of the rare few."

The Real and the Imagined
Trilogy

ISBN: 9798734987001

The Fiddler in the Night/Christian Fennell—1st edition.
The Real and the Imagined, Book Two

Any references to historical events, real people, or real places are used fictitiously. Names, characters, and places are products of the author's imagination.

Front cover art: Carolina Himmel
www.boutiquedeartedecarolinah.mitiendanube.com

F i r e n z e   B o o k s
www.firenzebooks.com

www.christianfennell.com

John and Nancy,
Kim and Liz, Dave and Julie.

"He had with him that selfsame rifle you see with him now, all mounted in german silver and the name that he'd give it set with silver wire under the checkpiece in latin: Et In Arcadia Ego."

~ Cormac McCarthy, *Blood Meridian*

THE FIDDLER IN THE NIGHT

PART ONE

A perfect silence.
Night coming.

The cold damp air, reaching and settling, and this man, he knew, and only by his own awareness did he know. Death coming.

Death waiting.

He lit a match. This unleashing of madness.

His name was Leonard. He was riding a bike. His arms held out to the sides of him, his mind never trapped by his own self, never buckling under the weight of what he should be, or shouldn't be, understanding the truth of himself, always, in this world, hard as that was, and of course, in this moment, too, riding a bike through the lonely continuum of time. He smiled at his knowing, where others couldn't, and he knew he was right, and always would be.

He rode on, his arms still there, to the sides of him, and he said, come, cover me. Gliding and dipping and soaring, and we do, going on and on, down a lonely long road, and free now, or at least so he thought. Free and wanting.

Free and needing.

And who among us would not say, such a person as this.

He turned and looked and he smiled. The old woman's jewelry, prizes of his glory, adorning him. Her lipstick, a mess now, covering his mouth. This sweet taste of his taking. He looked away and he reached his hands up to the breaking blue sky, and he said, yes yes yes, I am coming.

And in the darkness of the night, a young girl, endless in her time and lost to it, knows she'll dream soon, in a chair—her chair, an old armchair, threadbare, a blanket covering her. The warmth of the room with her and holding her still—holding her always. And she cried.

Tears she knows.

Tears she can't feel in these dreams of silence, of sunshine, dreams of a distance not yet known. Her mother there, always. Waiting.

She woke. A noise in the night. Her father asleep, passed out on the couch across from her, beneath a blanket she had put there.

The sound of the garage door. The car starting.

She got up and walked to the front window and watched the car driving away. And why wouldn't it be? And what could possibly be next? She didn't know. She looked behind her, at everything unseen and mostly unspoken. Her father, too, there in the quiet and lost to it. Taken. She turned back and looked to the darkness, and she knew, if she wanted to, she could see her own reflection, there in the glass before her, and waiting too.

She walked to the fireplace and stood for a while looking at the smoldering ash. She took up a long iron rod and poked at the burning ones. She put on another piece of firewood and climbed back onto her chair and pulled the blanket over her, and she wondered, would it always be like this? She didn't know, but she thought it might be. She closed her eyes and slept again, and it was running, always running, never there, never having, just running, and running now, in this falling of her emptiness.

Once again.

And he said, love under a big moon.

Of course, there is.

Why wouldn't there be?

And he looked up to that everyone's one big moon.

Probably was, and just forgotten.

Probably was.

He was walking, the car he'd stolen left at the side of the road. He stopped and looked around, and he thought, what else might be out there?

So many endless possibilities of strange and wonderful things.

He walked on, and he looked back up to that one big moon, and he reached up to it. You're mine, though, aren't ya? Every bit mine. Sooner or later, things'll get better. Ain't that right?

Ain't it now, said the moon back to him.

Why I'm here.

And never not here.

True enough, never not here.

And he was happy, walking, and he thought again, love under a big moon.

On a night such as this.

A boy and his mother were walking, not speaking, the low moving sky darkening. And it darkened more yet, such that it roofed the dirt and gravel road and the travelers upon the road in a manner that made this aged and distant Arcadian world appear constrictive, the travelers entrapped, a moment suggestive of past worlds—of those that had come before them. Lives harrowed in the dark vacancies of this place.

The boy stopped and toed a faded and blackened bloodstain.

Blood and dirt and nothing more than that.

A red-tailed hawk in the high winds.

His mother stopping, looking back.

He'd watched this hawk hunt before.

She looked too.

Dark smoke caught his eye, and he dropped the paper bag he was holding, an assortment of groceries and truck parts spilling onto the road.

A gunshot.

The hawk pulling up, calling to the breaking of the darkening quiet.

Jonathan McLean moved quickly through the trees and over the low stone wall. He ran across their pastures, his sixteen-year-old legs striding hard, his feet sturdy upon the uneven ground.

His father, Conor McLean, a tall man wearing a long dark coat with a hood, stood watching the flames of his own making, a blood-soaked sheep stretched over his right shoulder.

Fired blood, boiling and running.

Long streams of it.

Heavy black smoke drifting, and rancid.

The boy yelling.

Flames cracking bones.

The man cleared the sweat from his face, and thought, his own father would have done the same.

The fire exploding, embers and bits of flaming sheep pushing the boy back.

Not the father.

Madness, against the raging of madness, he called to his father.

The man looked partway over his shoulder, his dark squinting eyes burrowed deep, welled in this moment, impervious to the ways of reason and method, and he viewed the boy.

Jonathan knew his father's awareness of this place and time was often like nothing more than a quick glimpse of something that possibly was, or was not, there, and he yelled again, his voice drifting in the heavy black smoke, the sound of the sheep burning—these unholy sounds of hell itself, raging and settling, like some form of next plague here now, fear driving, fear eating, in our minds, these flames burning still.

The man turned back and tried to lift the sheep from his shoulder, but he could not, his weakness and exhaustion made visible, and he knew not to try again.

Jonathan covered his mouth and nose with his shirt and stepped forward.

The man leaning forward, the sheep falling from his shoulder. He dropped his shotgun and placed his large cold hands on his thighs, and he coughed, hard and deep, and he discharged a long spittle of blood.

Jonathan looked at the sheep at his father's feet, blood running from the shot holes in its neck, small particles of dirt drifting to the thick surface of the running blood, the blood soaking into the ground, claimed by the dirt as its own.

God's own bounty.

That's what he'd been told.

That's what he thought.

Pinching the spittle from his lip the man threw it away, and he looked at his son standing next to him, the boy only just shorter than the man. Burn em.

No.

They're poxed.

No, they're not.

Burn em.

No.

Boy—.

I won't.

Send em all back to God.

He'll do it, and Kathleen McLean placed her hand to her husband's face, and in that moment, everything they were was there before them—visible, as if marked as one by the stain of this life.

Come inside.

He had no fight, no will past hers.

So beautiful. Her hand upon his face. The madness in his eyes dissipating, and yet, there still, holding on, wanting, waiting, and needing more.

Jonathan picked up the Winchester twenty-gauge over-under shotgun and cracked the gun, an un-shot shell in the lower chamber, and he watched his parents walking up the winding dirt path, worn deep into the rocky grass hill, toward their small stone house.

Should they look back, either one, they'd see a boy standing alone outside of their love for one another, their love for him a separate love, a love just as deep and full but incapable all the same of saving him from the unavoidable and pending truth of all that is unseen and unanswerable, despite the intense desire otherwise that the last of his youngness still harbored.

He looked at the sheep at his feet, still breathing, its eye bulging large in its socket as if the uncertainty and fear pumping through its blood had crystallized it and turned it to glass. He put the gun to its head and pulled the trigger, the top of the sheep's head blowing forward, a sprayed trail of blood, brain matter, and bone fragment.

The sheep burning on.

The boy standing, watching.

Flames reaching.

A gun in his hand.

There, and ringing still, in this calling to madness.

Lived no more than twenty-five families of mostly Gaelic origin. This forgotten world. Here now, and before us. The heaviness of its vacancies, pulling and calling. These people, seemingly lost to the constant coming of it.

On three sides it was a long and steep drop to an unforgiving seaway, and where it adjoined with the mainland, it narrowed to less than a mile, and was from there a journey yet, not easily made to anywhere.

In the cool dampness of the dark death house, Jonathan reached for a string that hung overhead from a bare bulb. He pulled the string and a hard light was cast. He dropped the sheep to the black granite floor, worn smooth to a high gloss from a century and more of spilt blood and foot traffic. The walls, the same thick limestone of the house. Large exposed hemlock timbers supporting the trusses of the tin roof.

In the middle of the room next to the sheep was an opening in the granite floor filled with gravel. Above it hung a gun-style block and tackle with two double-sheave wooden pulleys and two hand-forged iron hooks. He pulled down one of the hooks and wrapped the rope around the sheep's legs and placed the hook back over the rope. With just a few hard pulls of the rope, the sheep hung, swinging, several feet above the floor.

From a row of butchery tools, set into designated holes along the back of a heavy table, he selected a bone-handled skinning knife. He walked to the sheep, pulled back its head, and opened its neck.

He squatted against the cold stone wall, and he watched the sheep bleeding out, and he thought, a covenant made and paid for.

Kathleen looked at her husband in the claw-footed tub before her, his white thin arms grasping his bony knees, startled and uncertain, and she washed him. She poured water over his head, rinsing him, and he rubbed the water from his eyes. She looked over her shoulder, at the silence holding memories between these walls. This falling of their days, faster than they should. Faster than they had any right to.

Jonathan looked to the other side of the hanging, blood-letting sheep, at two stools and a thick section of aged maple next to a cold rusted airtight stove, and he felt the vacancy of those stools now more than ever.

So many days, and so young, and he remembered.

He always would.

The flare of a wooden match, the good smell of it, his grandfather's words: What matters, boy, is what you do with your life, not what happens after you're dead.

Narrowed dark eyes behind thick blue pipe smoke: And how will you live your life?

With dignity.

Why?

No matter what happens, I'll always have it.

Cold thick fingers on his chin: In the old language?

Urram.

A smile and the smell of whiskey: Aye, boy, Urram.

Kathleen finished bathing Conor, and he stood, oversized and frail, and there was strength in his bones yet, some, but that was all there was.

Jonathan walked to the sheep and cut it open the length of its underside, his hands working inside the warmth of it, taking away its entrails.

Kathleen wiped clean the end of a hypodermic needle and drew ten milligrams of morphine from a small bottle. She put the bottle back on the night table and pushed down on the plunger, a steady stream of liquid squirting in the air. She pulled down Conor's pajama bottoms and inserted the needle into the muscle of his buttocks and plunged the morphine in.

She helped him into bed, and she kissed his forehead.

He watched his wife leaving, his breathing faint and shallow with a slight sporadic rattle. He closed his eyes, and he wondered, of the fires of hell. Of death coming. Death here. And he remembered, the flames of his purging.

Blood running—that burning.

Fear and death and that burning.

Kathleen dropped her bathrobe to the floor of the bathroom. She was slender, falling just on the side of tall, her thick honey-colored hair running to a length just past her shoulders. She put her hair up and stepped into a new tub venting steam from the hot running water. She leaned back and pulled her knees to her and looked at the room filled with a low soft light spilling out from a single shaded lamp, and in the absence of the moon and stars, the world beyond the thin glass of the window appeared to be a moving black, the drifting fog, a harbinger, perhaps, from an abyss unknown, of all things to be feared, real and imagined. She slid her legs beneath the water and leaned her head back and closed her eyes.

Beyond here was nowhere.

Not anymore. She was sure of it.

For her son too. She was sure of it.

Leonard stopped. There was a house set back from the road. He walked up the long gravel driveway.

The house was white stucco, cracked and chipped and stained with dirt. Tall weeds running up the walls.

To the right of the house, a clapboard garage the same color as the house.

He looked for a dog, or any sign of a dog. There wasn't one. Not that he could tell.

He walked toward the garage and stopped and looked back at the house. He reached for the garage door handle and pulled, the door lifting up from the ground toward him, a stack of aluminum folding chairs tipping over. He paused, holding the door handle, two weighted cylinders filled with rocks, one on either side of the door, swaying from thin strands of twisted wire.

A second-story light came on, and he let go of the handle, to see if the door would stay. It did, and he moved to the back of the house.

The back light came on, mosquitoes swarming the brightness. An old man wearing pajamas and a frayed, striped bathrobe appeared. His gray hair disheveled. His watery, hooded eyes squinting. A single-barrel shotgun in his hand. Who's there?

He pushed open the screen door to the hum of the evening heat and the sound of the mosquitoes bouncing off the glass of the small light. Well?

He stepped onto the porch boards, the screen door slapping shut behind him. I won't ask again.

He walked forward and Leonard stepped out from behind the house, wrapping his left arm around the man's neck. Shh, he said.

The old man eye's widening. He didn't struggle.

Leonard pressed the cold tip of a clip-blade knife to the man's throat. It's me.

The old man. Who?

The one ya been waitin for, and he ran the knife through the thin, slack skin of the old man's neck.

He looked at the blood, pooling on the broken patio stones. He looked at the closed screen door and the light behind the door.

An old woman called from the house. Horace?

He looked to the second-story window.

Is everything all right?

He stepped over the man bleeding out beneath him, and he entered the house.

The old woman appeared at the window, the soft bedroom light behind her highlighting the frailness of her thin frame beneath her long white nightgown. Horace?

Leonard appeared in the window, approaching the woman from behind, the old woman turning, and screaming.

Jonathan entered the mudroom spilling over with coats and boots and assorted other pieces of outer clothing, bits of tack and various outdoor implements and tools. He closed the door.

The gun rack mounted on the wall had an empty space just above a Lee-Enfield .303 and just below a Browning semi-automatic .22. He placed the Winchester there. Resting on the bottom of the gun rack was an SAA Colt .45 Peacemaker with a chipped pearl handle and several boxes of ammunition. He sat on a narrow wooden bench and removed his boots.

He scrubbed clean the blood covering his hands and lower arms, and he dried himself with a dish towel and removed a warm plate of stew from the oven. He picked up the waiting utensils from the counter and walked to the front room.

He sat in an armchair next to a large Rumford-style fireplace with a small fire burning, and he placed his plate of food and utensils before him on the wooden coffee table. He leaned forward and began to eat.

A carriage clock on the mantel ticked.

The warm light of the fire, and the flickering of tall heavy candles burning on the coffee table, highlighted Kathleen wrapped in a heavy white bathrobe sitting on the couch. The worn and tired-looking features of her face.

You're upset.

He didn't answer and he didn't look up.

Don't be.

She waited.

He said, why? Because he's sick?

She pulled her legs to her, on their sides in front of her, and she looked at her son. She looked at her paintings of the farm mounted on the wall next to the fireplace. This is all you know.

It's all I need to know, and he went back to eating.

No, she said quietly, and she watched him. It's not true.

He didn't look up.

There could be more. She paused again. At least, there could be, if we wanted there to.

He placed his utensils across his plate and stood. We'll figure it out.

Jonathan.

He stopped and looked back. Mom, please.

Check on your father before you go to bed.

All right, I will. Goodnight.

She watched him leave the room, and she looked at a painting on the wall, the three of them walking, their shadows stretching out long on the road before them.

Jonathan pushed open the bedroom door to the paneled room, small and shadowy with only a bedside lamp on. The air still and somewhat stale.

He entered the room and sat in a straight back chair next to the bed. On the bedside table were his father's pill bottles of different sizes, the hypodermic needle, the small bottle of morphine, a bowl filled with water. He looked at his father's pale face, his sunken chest, rising and falling, and he waited to see if he'd open his eyes.

He sat for a while.

He looked at his father's hand reaching out from under the covers, and he watched him try to speak. He leaned closer.

Keep an eye on her.

I will, Da, I promise. He waited to see if his father would speak again, and he looked at his father's hand, thin and bony and aged, long crooked fingers. He lifted it. It was cold. And he put it back under the covers.

The boy stood and walked to the door and looked back. He waited again, and he closed the door behind him.

The warmth of the fire surrounded Kathleen's coiled body like some form of healing she wished she could will deep to her bones, or beyond, should such a place exist. She was tired, and she leaned her head back and closed her eyes.

Leonard woke in the night and sat up in the old couple's bed, and he looked at the woman beneath the window on the floor, her nightgown soaked in blood, a long stream of it having run from her. He turned on the bed and placed his boots on the well waxed hardwood floor, and he lowered his head and closed his eyes and ruffled his hair. He looked up at an antique vanity desk across from the bed.

He sat on the chair and opened a jewelry box and ran his fingers through it, an old broach, a charm bracelet, several pairs of earrings, a pearl necklace, and matching pearl earrings. He fisted it all and put it in his coat pocket. He looked back at the old woman, and he stood and walked to her.

He squatted and took her left hand into his, sizing up her diamond ring and wedding band. He tried to pull them off. They wouldn't come. He pulled harder. He took his knife out and opened the blade. He folded back the other fingers of her hand and pressed her hand to the floor and pushed the blade through the crunch of bone. He slid the rings off the backside of her freed finger and dropped the finger to the floor. He cleaned the blade on her nightgown and folded the knife closed. He tilted his head, staring at the old woman's opened eyes, and he wondered, what was in there still?

Anything?

Doubt it.

Would it make a difference?

Probably not.

I bet they're thankin ya?

Bet they are.

If they could.

Why wouldn't they?

She seemed like someone's nice old grandma.

He stood and pocketed the rings, and he walked down the stairs.

Like they'd lived here a long time.

I guess.

And they might have been happy.

Possibly. But I didn't put em in my path, someone else done that. And if there's a reason for that, there's a reason for me.

No doubt. Everything else is just made up, ain't it?

True enough, just made up. Except I ain't, and I never will be.

He lifted the kettle from the stove and poured out the water and refilled it. He placed it back on the stove, turned the element on, and looked in the fridge. He closed it, and he walked out the back door.

He stepped over the dead old man and the patio stone blood and walked to the garage. He lifted the garage door and looked at the cluttered mess. There wasn't even a car. Nothing much at all.

He walked back to the house, up the stairs, and inside.

He lifted the whistling kettle from the stove and searched the cupboards until he found a jar of instant coffee. He made a strong mug of black coffee and carried it to the table. He sat and crossed his legs and took a sip. He lit a cigarette, smoked, and he drank his coffee.

Conor turned in the bed and stood slowly. He made it to the window and put his hands to either side of the frame to support himself, and he looked to the darkness and what he saw there, and beyond that, and what he wanted most.

A cold dark hole.

In a box.

This fate of his coming soon, and yet, he did not know hers, although he should have, for why wouldn't they be the same? Of course, they would. The two of them as one, and always having been, especially now, in these long cold nights of their certainties.

With the hood of his oilskin Mac pulled over his head, Jonathan walked in the hard morning rain from the house to the barn. He opened the man-door and stepped inside. The animals stirred and rustled. He dropped his hood and switched on the overhead lights and somewhere pigeons fluttered and flew to a perch overhead. The sound of the rain striking the large tin roof echoed throughout the barn. The smell of ancient timbers, worn floorboards, aged and wet white pine siding, the animals, slightly soiled straw bedding, the feed, and the steady cool draft of damp air, all blended to one smell that was both familiar and welcoming to him.

The right side of the barn housed the Katahdin sheep, what was left, all of them congregated toward the far end. Across the wide walkway was the tack and feed room. Next to it, a Holstein cow. Stalled separately, three quarter horses, all mares. The tallest at fifteen-and-a-half hands was a beautiful hunter bay with well-groomed black points. The other two were sorrel cutters, standing between fourteen and fifteen hands.

He entered the sheep pen and walked to the large center doors. He unbolted and unlatched and pushed them open to the rainy darkness. Beyond the doors was a barnyard corral. He didn't pasture the sheep due to the rain, and he fed and watered them there. He walked toward the Holstein and entered the stall and saw the tin cup on the milking stool. He hung it on a nail above the stool. He milked the Holstein and with only a partially filled pail of milk, he left the stall and exited the barn.

He collected the eggs from the chicken coop and started across the compound toward the house.

The basement was damp and cool, and he pulled on an overhead light. From a stack of empty egg cartons, he removed one and placed the eggs he collected into it. He opened the fridge marked eggs and put the carton inside. He poured the milk into a ten-gallon stainless steel milk can with a spigot sitting on a wooden stool next to a large utility sink, and he rinsed the pail out. He turned the light off and walked from the basement back to the barn.

He tacked up the bay they called Destiny, and he took her from the stall, her hooves clipping on the wide worn floorboards, the sound hanging long and lonely in the cold barn air.

Kathleen stood at the front room window watching her son ride over the empty pastures, his hands folded over the pommel, his shoulders hunched forward, his head down, such that he and the horse appeared silhouetted as one against the rainy blue-black of the early morning, engaged in what looked to be like the entrusted burden of carrying upon their backs the death of yesterday's darkness.

And she spoke her son's name to the coming of the day.

Daddie?

She waited.

I made some tea and toast, and she placed them on the coffee table. She sat in a chair across from her father, and she waited for him to wake.

He didn't move.

You should eat something.

He opened his eyes, and he squinted them closed again. He rubbed his face. Thanks. He sat up and rested his arms on his legs. He looked at Rachael. I overslept.

That's all right.

Did you have something?

The same, tea and toast.

He sipped his tea.

Daddie.

Yeah.

Last night, someone took the car.

They what?

They took the car. I heard the garage door and then I saw them drive away.

Jesus Christ.

Daddie!

Sorry. He took a bite of toast. That's okay, they won't get far.

They won't?

Nope. Ignition relay is shot, among other things. Did you see which way they turned?

Right.

Okay, good. We'll look for it later, or maybe tomorrow. We've got that woman coming today.

Rachael didn't answer.

He looked at her. It'll be okay.

She nodded.

Start your schoolwork. I'll be there in just a minute.

Jonathan dismounted at the low stonewall running alongside the road. He tethered the horse to a heavy hanging branch. He watched the Doc's gray Saxon Eighty-Eight drive by, sending remnants of the bag and its contents he'd dropped on the road yesterday whirling to either side of the dewy road.

He searched through the wet debris looking for truck parts and usable food. He couldn't find either one. He looked back toward the house and watched the car driving up their long gravel driveway, the sun highlighting the polish of the car, reflecting from the windows and chrome, and he tried not to think of his dad.

He rode the tree line next to the road and where the woods began to widen, he reined the horse and entered the woods at the mouth of a trail. He took up his binoculars and panned the trees.

He kicked the horse, and he moved down the trail.

It was quiet, the first light of day penetrating the treetops, giving the forest the appearance of a damp and dripping canopy. Everywhere were fallen and broken trees in varying degrees of decay, some caught up in standing trees and waiting to fall yet. Widow-makers, his father called them.

He dismounted and picked up a stick and walked toward three sheep grazing in the woods, and he herded them toward the field.

The sky was starting to break apart disclosing a distant and nearly forgotten shade of washed blue. Jonathan stood the horse and with his hands folded over the pommel, the sheep grazing before him, he surveyed the land of Urram Hill, and it was these moments now, he liked best, everything still and quiet, with nothing before him he could not understand.

The farthest point of the farm ran ten acres across in its width. A thin line of trees followed the road back to their house and beyond, forming the southwest border. From the woods moving toward the middle of the point was the family cemetery, a white picket fence corralling hundreds of tombstones, all the same shape and size and cut from the same type of stone. The land to the northeast followed the line of a high cliff back past the house and farther yet, such that it appeared as if the farm on this side was bordered only by the sky.

He looked at the graveyard, and he thought of his grandfather. He thought of his father.

Keep an eye on her.

He leaned from the saddle and unlatched and swung open the paddock door from the pasture side. He rode behind the corralled herd and moved them through the open gate and drove them toward the farthest pasture where he'd left the other sheep grazing. As he rode, he watched the Doc's car leaving.

Walking from the house with a laundry basket, the wind pushing on her, crows circling, Kathleen watched Jonathan herd the sheep, up and over the rolling pastures, weathered and crumbling dry stonewalls encased in thistles and other common field weeds rising and falling and intersecting like some well-thought-out testimony to purpose and will. She remained standing, long past the point of his riding from her sight. The crows there, some having settled on the clothesline, and watching too. Go on, she told them. We don't need any more of your news. Not that kind. Not the kind you'll bring. Go on, she said again.

She picked up the basket and walked back to the house.

Rachael told the state-sponsored woman, she came out there. The woman looked at the house.

I saw her from my window. It was dark, but there was a big moon, and she was wearing her long white nightgown.

Your mother went into the garage?

Yes, said Rachael, and she pushed off the ground with her foot, pulling back on the chains, the swing going, the rusted chains squeaking.

The too dark garage, afraid to turn the light on, afraid to wake them, and so she stumbled, even though she knew where it was—exactly where it was, that which she had come for, and would not put off.

Not anymore.

Did you see her come out of the garage?

Rachael looked at the garage, the squeak of the chains slowing.

Rachael?

She looked at the woman. She had something in her hand, but I couldn't see what it was.

In the dark she reached the workbench and placed a pitcher of lemonade and ice on it. She bent down and looked beneath the bench, her hand searching, and then finding, that which she had come for. She struggled to lift it with one hand and bent over more, using both hands to place it on the bench.

The swing was hardly moving now, just drifting, slowly, back-and-forth, as if there was a big moon up there, that very same moon, and it was dark, and it was quiet, and she was alone and waiting. And she'd say, Momma.

Rachael looked at the woman, at her nice hair. Her nice clothes.

Your momma?

Yes. She looked at the house. I think Daddie's upset because he was supposed to be watching her.

Is that what he said?

No, but I know he was.

Why?

Because he left his job so he could.

He was a teacher?

Yes, the only one and he taught us all.

Who's the teacher now?

It's a lady, but I don't go, so I don't know. My daddie teaches me here.

He does?

Yes, mostly, but not every day.

Was your daddie sleeping when your momma went outside?

He didn't wake up until we heard her fall in the hallway.

She left the garage?

Yes, but she was in there a long time.

Sitting on the high wooden stool, her legs crossed, she sipped her mixed drink of lemonade and antifreeze. And in the dim blue light of the moon slipping through the side door window, she stared into the darkness of new hope, and she began to hum the song, You Are My Sunshine.

She hummed on, her foot tapping on, the music in her head—playing on, and she forced down another sip.

And she whispered to the darkness, you'll never know, dear, how much I love you.

Rachael stopped the swing. I should get supper goin.

I can give you a hand.

That's all right.

No, I'd like to, if that's okay?

Did your daddie talk to you about your momma?

Not too much, said Rachael. Would you like a cup of tea?

Yes, please.

I'll put the kettle on.

Thank you.

You're welcome. He just said, did I know she died of a broken heart?

A broken heart?

Yes, that's what he said. Because the world made her sad.

I'm sorry.

That's okay. But it wasn't just the world that made her sad.

It wasn't?

No. She told me why.

She did?

Yes. She said, sometimes she got sad because another world, not this one, another one, would come and settle upon her. But I wasn't to worry because it would never come for me. She said she just knew, and I would be okay. She promised.

She said that?

Yes.

She promised?

Yes.

Do you worry about that?

She looked at the woman. The state-sponsored woman.

Rachael?

She heard her name, but she wasn't there, she was on her swing. Under a big moon.

That very same moon.

In the dark, in the quiet, waiting.

That calling. That pulling. The chains squeaking.

Standing at the top of a large outcropping of granite rock, shadows of big birds flying, Leonard sighted the land, a warm breeze coming. And he thought, that was enough, more than enough, for him to know he was right for wanting to be here, in this place now.

He closed his eyes and tilted his head back and he let the breeze take him.

And it did.

A coyote watching.

More shadows of big birds flying.

Conor coughed.

Kathleen woke.

He coughed more.

She sat around and poured a glass of water. She nudged his shoulder. Conor. She nudged him again.

He opened his eyes and tried to push himself up.

She held the glass to his mouth and tipped it back. I'll get your shot.

Not yet fully awake, Kathleen felt her anger returning, anger she thought had passed and gone long ago, given way to the acceptance of what they had become, the gutted and hollowed sleeves of that which they once were, and worse yet, of what she thought they might become. Anger nurtured by her own shortcomings and self-betrayal, seeing always still, in his sick and ruined self: the boy, the man, the husband, the father, he once was.

She couldn't get back to sleep, and so she watched her husband sleeping. She leaned to him. Conor.

He didn't wake.

Can you remember? And she ran her finger down the hard outline of his weathered face. All those years when we were just young? She kissed him, in the dark, and she put her head next to his, this shell of the man she loved. She closed her eyes and she took him in. She closed her eyes and she took him in, all of him, that long ago boy, and she did not see the tear that came to his eye. She did not see the lessening of him yet. And she remembered. That time, not the day, not the season, not the year, just the feel of his finger writing small words on her back. Words, she thought, she was lost to still.

Beneath the light of the moon and the stars, Jonathan swung a sledgehammer onto a metal wedge, splitting another block of hardwood. The fire behind him burning high and hot and reaching far into the night. He picked up the wedge and set it into one of the halves of the split block and brought it down again. He set the wedge onto the other half and split it. He leaned the sledgehammer against the log and picked up the chunks of split wood and tossed them onto the fire, a spray of embers reaching to the darkness, and beyond, and farther yet, in search of some unknown celestial map of this world, setting alight the way of the future. A future this night that was his, and his alone.

Jonathan?

Kathleen woke.

Conor tried to sit up.

She put her hand to his forehead. He was hot and he was sweating and she told him, he's still out there.

He looked at his wife.

Try to get back to sleep.

He's upset?

He'll be fine.

He leaned his head back and closed his eyes. You were right.

Oh?

There should be more to this than just what we inherit.

I inherited you, didn't I?

There wasn't much choice, was there? Besides, I thought it was the other way around?

It was, and she moved her head next to his.

Every day, he said.

Every day?

Those days when we were just young.

We've had a full life. And now there were tears in her eyes.

There's still Jonathan.

Is there?

He's a good boy. You'll be okay.

Will we?

You know I'd take you with me, if I could. We might find a field up there like your father's?

That'd be nice.

Yes, it would.

They closed their eyes and slept, the two of them together, dreaming as one, of those days when they were still just young, under their forever skies.

Death waits patiently.

Jonathan swung the sledgehammer onto the metal wedge, splitting the last block of hardwood. He was shirtless. Sweating. Tired, he leaned the sledgehammer against the log bench and pitched the last of the wood he'd split onto the fire.

A fire to light the way to what? He didn't know.

Eternity is not a question for the young.

And so he burned the night like a scream for help, consumed as he was by a darkness he did not understand. A darkness fueled by his hatred and inability to comprehend the events of his life now laid bare before him, like so many slow deaths of familiar and constant sounds and the awareness that comes with new sounds, that once heard are difficult to ignore and harder yet to contain. Sounds that burn and blind, leading him to this field alight as it was with the full glory of the stars and the moon such that it be a perfect night for the taking of a stand, yelling: Fuck you, God.

Kathleen opened her eyes, momentarily uncertain and confused. Her eyes adjusting to the darkness, she looked at Conor, awake next to her, his left-hand pressed flat to the blankets, his other hand attempting to steady the hypodermic needle above a vein in his hand. The chamber of the needle filled with only air.

She laid her hand upon his, her tears falling, and she whispered, wait for me, and in the dim blue light of the night breaking through the open window, touching, and holding to them, adjoining them, she pressed her hand down upon his.

Leonard stopped walking. He took a drag from his cigarette and flicked it to the side of the road. He was wearing the old woman's jewelry, several necklaces, clip-on earrings, bracelets, and rings on his pinky fingers. He looked to the sky. To the moon. He squinted. His red-rimmed eyes milky white and faded blue. There was a tattoo on the nape of his neck, the opened and blood dripping jaws of some beast, a dog perhaps, from some other place and time. And just like that, he began to soar, tucking and weaving, his arms held out to the sides of him, the lipstick and jewelry being all that kept him here, otherwise, he would fly away, like a big bird, the biggest one, over the treetops, and in the wind.

No games here along fences.

That's what he thought, and he flew on—on and on.

The biggest one.

An eagle.

Soaring and happy. Spiraling. Spiraling over a long hard road, and he said, yes yes yes, I am here now.

PART TWO

Holly soaked in a tub, her body immersed in warm water that would not free her. Falling. Again and again. Falling. Like she'd read in a book one time. One of her mother's.

Falling, from the sad sloping shoulders of this world.

Fuck it, she thought. She'd take his damn beatings, and more of them, and keep trying. No matter what, keep trying. And she promised herself she would.

Or die trying.

She slid back in the tub and submerged herself, her eyes closed, not breathing, remaining still in that silence where her dreams of herself as a young girl lived.

She tried to stay there, as long as she could, the brilliance of the sunlight finding her standing on the dusty wooden porch of their store, looking up at her father, endless in her reaching.

She opened her eyes. She needed air. And yet she stayed under longer, delaying the coming back to the stench and filth of this world, that was so much stronger than everything she could conjure. Stronger than... and she burst above the water, taking in air. And she thought, what if she was wrong? What if it would always be like this?

The whistle of the kettle startled her. She heard it stop. Rooke making coffee.

She exited the bathroom wearing her bathrobe, her hair up in a towel. She tried to walk past him, standing with his coffee in his hand, leaning against the counter, watching.

I made coffee.

Good for you.

He reached out and grabbed her arm and forced her onto a chair at the kitchen table, the towel falling, her long wet hair hanging before her face.

He looked at the spilt coffee on the floor. Why do ya always gotta make everything so damn difficult? He sat at the table across from her. Shit costs money. People come here, they win or lose, we make money. They get drunk and horny, we make money. What's so bad about that?

She moved the hair from the front of her face and she sat up in the chair, her back straight, her eyes searching his. What do you want?

He sipped his coffee, looking at her smooth skin, her fine features, her full lips. The top of her breasts—so smooth, too, and round and white. We're goin to the Lamplight tonight, that's all, and I don't want any more of your shit. Understand?

Got it.

He looked more.

She narrowed her eyes. You better fucking not. Don't even try.

He smiled.

That it?

Yup. That's it.

She got up and walked to the door, her bare feet stepping on the sticky boozy floorboards. She reached the front door and waited.

Rooke appeared and bent down and locked an ankle bracelet on her, and she walked to her small trailer, dragging a heavy chain staked to a post in the center of the dead lawn. She sat on the trailer step and picked up her smokes and lighter and lit one. She put them back on the step and took the cigarette from her lips. She exhaled and looked at Rooke, still standing at the open door. She flipped him the finger, and he smiled, and he walked back inside and closed the door.

She'd make her own damn coffee, thank you very much, and she flicked her cigarette away and walked into the trailer.

She picked up a book and she sat on the narrow bed. She read and drank her coffee, waiting out the day, not getting dressed—what would be the point in that?

She'd drag out every minute. Holding on to it, and not letting go. The slowing of time. The killing of what was coming next.

If she found she was getting too lost in her reading, she'd stop and just sit and think, and if she got too lost in her thoughts, she'd stop herself from drifting back to those days, when life wasn't this. When she was just a little girl.

She looked at the house through the small window behind her. She'd be putting on those shitty slutty clothes soon enough. Fuck it, and she went back to her reading, but she couldn't focus, and she threw the book across the room and she watched it hit the trailer wall and fall to the floor.

She brought her knees to her and put her face there, and she listened to the sound of the wind in the trees. For a long time. She started to breathe to the rhythm of it, and she felt better. And now she heard herself saying, for the hundredth time that day, one day.

One day coming soon.

Together they walked the side of the road, Rachael and her father, this man Peter English.

Will it take long? Rachael asked.

No, her father told her.

They walked more.

He looked at his daughter. Getting tired?

No, it's okay. I'm fine.

It can't be much farther.

She took his hand.

We needed the exercise, anyway, didn't we?

She looked up at her father. Probably you a little more than me, wouldn't ya say?

He laughed and said, yes, my beautiful little smart-ass, me a little more than you.

They walked on, for there is always love under a big sky, too, said both of their hearts to one another at the same time.

The smoke of a swinging censer, drifting, and dissipating, in the cold damp morning air. A death march in black carrying a casket over pastures, the hard soles of the pallbearers' leather shoes, sinking and sliding, in patches of wet packed field mud. This re-tracing of ancestral steps. Singing, I Am at Ease, low and soft, as if not to tempt fate. Some just humming, in this marching of their time coming.

The priest at the gravesite waited, the others surrounding the open grave.

Six men stepped forward and picked up three heavy ropes stretched over the grave. The pallbearers placed the casket there, and as the priest began to pray in Latin, the men lowered the casket into the ground.

Kathleen stepped forward. Jonathan helping her. She bent over and picked up a handful of dark graveyard dirt from a large pile next to the grave. She stood looking down into the hole, and she said, may He always hold you in the hollow of His hand. She looked at the surrounding silent faces solemn in their mourning. She looked at Jonathan. She looked back at the dark hole, and she leaned forward and whispered, wait for me, and she released the dirt, and with it, everything she was. Had been. Had never not been.

Rachael watched her father working on the car. She looked around. She was never at ease in wide open spaces. She heard the hood close, and she looked at her father cleaning his hands on a rag. Can we go?

Yes, he said, and they got in the car. He started it up and pulled onto the road.

She looked out the window.

At what?

At everything so seemingly foreign to her and unsettling.

Why?

She didn't know. She wished she did.

A gathering of men, some with their suit jackets still on, some without, stood lingering and talking on the porch and front lawn just beyond the porch. At the entrance to the pathway from the driveway was a clach cuid fir weighing two hundred and twenty-five pounds, resting on a small pillar fifty-two inches in height. There was a corresponding pillar for receiving the stone on the other side of the pathway. A stone set there hundreds of years ago by Samuel McLean, the founder of Urram Hill. A stone used still, for sport, for amusement, the testing of manhood with sons pitted against sons, sons against fathers, and for more than a time or two, the settling of wagers.

A tall man standing next to Jonathan looked at the stone. What about you? Have ya had ago?

Jonathan looked at the stone.

Go on then, said a very large man sitting on the porch and flicking his hand out toward the stone. No time like the present.

Right, said another man.

Someone took Jonathan's drink and another man removed Jonathan's suit jacket.

He had no interest in this, none at all. But he knew how it would go. They wouldn't be put off.

They moved him toward the stone, and he rolled up his sleeves.

When'd your own da do it? someone in the gathering crowd asked.

At the mention of the boy's father, a collective pause fell over the men.

Seventeen, said Jonathan.

The men raised their glasses. To Conor.

The very best of who we are, said another man.

To Conor, they said again, and they tipped back their drinks.

There hasn't been a McLean yet that hasn't lifted that stone. Isn't that right, boy?

What are you, then? someone else asked.

Sixteen.

The large man on the porch stood. I have a fiver that says he won't do it.

Jonathan's uncle, Angus Edmunds, stepped forward. I'll take that wager. He looked at Jonathan, and he smiled. He looked at the men. I'll cover every goddamn one of ya, if ya the balls.

Done, said one man.

Sixteen? said another man. Put me down.

Me too.

I'm in.

Right then, said Angus, it's on.

39

The men moved closer, gathering around Jonathan and the stone.

Angus put his hand to his mouth and spat some chew there. Not to worry, he said to Jonathan, and he winked. We just need to limber these arms up a wee bit. He took hold of Jonathan's forearm and rubbed the chew there. He did the same with the other arm.

Jonathan squatted and pressed his chest to the stone, wrapping his arms around it. At the back of the stone his fingers were several inches apart.

Angus leaned forward. Ya need to get your fingers locked. Reposition it.

Jonathan stood and looked at the stone and he placed his hands on it and gave it a slight twist counterclockwise. He squatted and tried again, his fingers just touching. He pressed his chest forward and his fingers began to interlock. He pressed forward harder, the right side of his face pressed against the stone, and he locked his fingers.

He closed his eyes and took a deep breath and pushed up from the ground with the full force of his legs and back while squeezing the stone with his arms and wide shoulders. He raised the stone off the platform and took a small step back, the tremendous weight of the stone causing it to fall from his chest to his lap, the edges of the stone digging into his thighs. He held it. He tried to reposition the stone higher and managed to lift it enough to get it off his thighs and more onto his stomach. He began to move forward in a slow strained duck walk.

By God, said one of the men watching, would you look at that?

Angus walked next to him. That's it, boy, keep going. It's not far.

And him just sixteen, said another man.

He's gotta make it there yet, said the very large man sitting on the porch.

Angus told him, lean it against the pillar.

And he did. His face deep red, his lungs sucking in air, his strength completely spent.

Right, said Angus, demonstrating while speaking, ya hav'ta arch your back like this, then roll it up onto your chest until it's higher than the post and step forward and let her go.

Jonathan nodded.

He leaned closer to Jonathan. Do it for ya da.

Jonathan looked at Angus. No, he said, and he tried to catch his breath. I'll do it so I never have to lift this goddamn thing again.

The men close enough to have heard all laughed.

The large man on the porch stood and called out, you're not get'n any stronger just standin there like that, get it up.

A short bald man sitting on the porch next to the large man said, didn't ya just bet a fiver he wouldn't do it?

The hell with the fiver.

Jonathan's mother and several other women stood watching from the narrow French doors that opened to the porch.

Jonathan began to position himself, and the men fell silent. He did as Angus instructed and rolled the heavy stone up onto his chest while arching his back. He gave the stone a last lift with his arms and shoulders and just before he leaned forward to let it fall, a protruding edge caught against the lip of the pillar, stopping the stone from coming to rest. It teetered, and he bent quickly to press the stone against his chest before it fell. He held it. He repositioned his arms to the lower sides of the stone and with all his will and determination trumping his lack of available strength, he rolled the stone up and onto the pillar.

The men cheered, many of them lifting their glasses in the air. To Jonathan.

They came forward and congratulated him, and as they walked past Angus, they pressed their fivers into his hand, and not one of the men, in offering their congratulations to Jonathan, referred to him as boy.

The women entered the house, Kathleen lingering at the open door.

Well, said Angus, thirty-six men and in this hand is one hundred and eighty dollars. It warms the heart, doesn't it? He slipped the money under the stone. You earned it. He put his hand to Jonathan's shoulder. You've made your da proud this day.

At the front door, Jonathan saw his mother still standing, looking back at him. She smiled.

Angus looked too. Goodness, he said. He paused, just looking. Such a beautiful girl. The bones of a bird.

Jonathan hadn't heard his grandfather's expression for his mother in a long time.

All of us boys and then a girl, finally. So beautiful, and yet so fragile. He loved her though, didn't he? He looked at Jonathan. Course your da, too. Everyone did. And he never had to worry, not with Conor. He looked back at Kathleen. They were never apart, you know, not since the very beginning. Not that I can remember.

The sound of a fiddle being tuned drifted from the house and everyone began to fall silent. They waited and as the first clear sad notes of the Michael Keane tune, 'A Lament for My Father,' drifted outside, the men either moved inside or gathered around the open doors.

I believe you might be needed.

Jonathan walked up the porch stairs, and when the first of the men saw him, they stepped aside, tapping others on the shoulder, who turned and looked and stepped aside.

Jonathan walked to his mother. He stopped and extended his hand.

She took it and they looked at one another, their shattered hearts entwining, sinking together, and they danced in this sorrow, her head on his shoulder, their feet moving slowly over the dark worn floorboards.

Jonathan put his Mac over his suit and walked to the barn. He tacked up Destiny, and he rode over the wet rolling pastures of Urram Hill.

He stopped at the graveyard and looked at the open grave. At the pile of dark graveyard dirt. He dismounted, and with the reins held in one hand, he picked up a handful of the dirt and dropped in the hole. Travel well, Da.

He remained there a long time, just standing, in this greater vacancy yet.

She stood at the door opening of the trailer dressed in a short tight black dress with a low neckline. Black high heels. She watched Rooke back the pickup to the trailer and hook it up. He walked to the door and put up the stair. Time to go. She stepped inside and he closed and locked the door.

The house was quiet. The furniture moved back into place and the dishes done and put away.

Mom?

He walked to the fridge and opened it. He closed it. He walked into the living room. She wasn't there. He walked back into the kitchen and stood at the foot of the stairs. Mom? He waited, and he walked into the mudroom and put his boots and coat back on.

He walked toward the barn and past it, following a narrow path through a thin line of trees. At the edge of the high cliff, he saw his mother sitting on a large rock overlooking the seaway.

They sat together, the seagulls before them, circling, calling to the dying day. A bald eagle, close to them, descending in large easy loops on massive wings. The Kingfishers, too, calling from their nests wedged into the jagged rocks of the cliff.

I can't remember a moment without him. And I'm so very grateful for that. She looked at her son. And for you.

We'll be all right.

That's what he said.

We will, I promise.

She put her head on her son's shoulder, and together they watched the sun falling beyond the fast-moving waters of the seaway, running between these two high rocky shorelines, reaching long in their sights, and farther yet, toward a great estuary, and the possibility of other worlds beyond that. Always waiting, and remaining unknown.

This is your place now, she said.

He thought of his father's words, keep an eye on her, and his uncle's, the bones of a bird, and he said again, we'll be okay. You'll see, we will. I promise.

In an open back room of the bar, Rooke and several other men were playing cards. Rooke folded his hand and poured a glass of whiskey. A fat man with black slicked back hair and a white wrinkled suit and square pink-tinted glasses walked up to Rooke and leaned over. His name was Harvey. She's free now, said Harvey, and he dropped a twenty on the table.

Rooke leaned back in his chair and watched the fat man walking away. If you don't get it done in thirty minutes, you don't get it done. Understand?

The man waved his hand in the air as he walked away. He stopped and looked back. In thirty minutes, I can get around the world and back, and then some.

Some of the men looked and laughed.

Personally, I don't give a shit where ya go, said Rooke, you got thirty minutes. And don't make a mess of it, like the last time. Any more of that sick shit and I'll ban your fat ass for lifetime.

Not to worry, said the fat man. I'm in a mood for love, and little else. He walked out of the room and through the quiet bar and out the door.

A sound in the night woke Jonathan. He turned his bedside light on and waited for his eyes to adjust. He sat around on the bed and placed his feet on the cold floorboards. He waited to see if he could hear anything else. He couldn't, and he stood. He reached for his pants hanging over the back of a straight back chair, and he slipped them on. He walked out of his bedroom and down the dark hallway. He stopped at the top of the stairs and listened. Nothing. He walked down the stairs and stopped and listened again. He turned the kitchen light on. Everything appeared as it should. Nothing missing. He walked through the rest of the house turning on lights, looking and listening. Still nothing. He returned to the foot of the stairs and looked toward the mudroom. The gun rack door was ajar. He entered the room and opened the door fully. Both rifles and the shotgun were still there. Before he closed the door, he noticed the Colt .45 Peacemaker with the chipped pearl handle was missing. He left the mudroom, climbed the stairs, and ran down the hallway to his mother's room. He opened the door. She wasn't there. He ran back down the hallway, down the stairs, and out the door. He called to the darkness, Mom? He stepped farther into the night and called again.

Most of the light and sounds of the day were lost to a hard rain and a cold wind pushing in from the northeast.

A Celtic-like mist, drifting.

Eyes straining to see more.

Jonathan and the constable stood next to one another at the edge of the cliff in the first pasture nearest to the barn, their horses tethered behind them, the sounds of the seaway below them. The hood of Jonathan's Mac was pulled up over his head. The constable, a dark police issue rain poncho with the hood pulled over his head.

Jonathan looked at him. You think she's out there.

I didn't say that.

No, but it's what you're thinking.

I don't know what I'm thinking, so I don't see how you could. Is cucaidhchumhach am bron, he said to Jonathan in Gaelic.

Jonathan was unsure of the translation.

Sorrow is a powerful instrument.

If she's out there, someone did it.

You ever see this someone?

No, but you think it's a coincidence she's gone missing the same night someone broke into our house?

No, I don't. No more than I do her going missing the night of Conor's wake. But I'll tell you what, we'll find your mother, or her body, and when we do, it'll tell us everything we need to know.

And in the meantime, whoever did it will be gone.

This person, did they take anything other than your father's gun?

No.

How do you know your mother didn't take it?

Together they turned and watched a rider approaching. He stopped next to the constable.

We found signs of a camp.

Where?

In the woods by the graveyard.

And?

Nothin much. Signs of a fire and some food wrappers.

Any truck parts? Jonathan asked.

Truck parts?

I dropped a new starter for it on the road the other day.

The constable looked at Jonathan. For the pickup?

Jonathan nodded.

No, nothing like that, said the man on horseback.

The constable mounted his horse and looked at Jonathan. Coming?

You go on ahead.

The constable moved alongside of Jonathan. Why was your mother in such a hurry to sell?

Sell?

She talked to Angus, at your father's wake.

She said she wanted to sell?

Asked if he'd be interested.

Jonathan mounted Destiny and the constable rode up next to him. I wish you wouldn't do this. It won't take us more than a day or two to find her.

I'm not staying. I'm going.

Let me send someone with you.

I can cover well enough where I need to on my own, thanks.

If you see anything, or anyone, get back here and let us know. I mean that, Jonathan.

Jonathan turned Destiny and started to ride toward the house. He stopped and looked back. Constable Stanley.

The constable and the other rider stopped and looked back.

When you see Angus, tell him the place isn't for sale.

You can tell him your own self when you get back.

Jonathan dismounted and swung open the pasture gate. He walked Destiny to the large double doors of the barn and opened both. He walked her to her stall and tethered her there.

He opened all the stall doors and began to fill the feed troughs.

In the tack room, he picked up a saddlebag and put it over his shoulder. He pulled the hood of his Mac back over his head and walked out of the barn to the house.

He moved through the house filling the saddlebag with a change of clothes, the money he won lifting the manhood stone, a compass, and a box of strike-anywhere matches. He left the saddlebag on the kitchen table and walked down into the basement and switched on the light. At the pantry, he took down a jar of sweet onions, some dried jerky, and a jar of pickled eggs. He was about to leave and he stopped, reaching back and unhooking a small wineskin.

He walked up the stairs and loaded the food into the saddlebag. He walked to the sink and filled the wineskin with cold water.

In the mudroom, he opened the gun rack and picked up the box of 20-gauge shells. He took down the over-under and closed the door. He reached back and opened the gun rack door and took down the shotgun shoulder strap hanging from a wooden peg on the backside of the door. He closed the gun rack door, opened the outside door, and stepped into the rain. He closed and locked the door and walked to the barn.

In the barn he pulled his hood down and walked toward Destiny. He placed the saddle bag over the horse and bound the bag and the saddle together. He untied Destiny's reins and walked her to the open barn doors and stood amongst the other animals looking at the hard rain falling, and the cold day hanging over Urram Hill.

All those McLeans, he thought, and now his father, and possibly his mother too. He mounted Destiny, kicked her hard, and rode toward the road.

PART THREE

The rain stopped and the quiet woke Leonard. The sounds of men shouting back and forth from horses, and the small boats dragging the seaway, had also stopped. He raised himself onto his elbows and stretched his head back and looked out the dusty garage window where cobwebs hung loose in the corners, the faded white paint of the wooden frame, mostly flaked and fallen away.

He sat upright in the box of the truck and lit a cigarette and watched the slow death of the day and the darkness becoming whole. He smoked, and he thought of what? Of the will of men and their endless search for redemption, where there was none.

Not that he could tell.

So proud in their knowing, in that which they could not know.

Their hearts emptying. Slowly. Over time. This endless fear of not knowing.

That's what it was, he thought.

The one thing they couldn't let themselves know.

Never.

Not today.

Not ever.

He looked again out the window to the damp gray day. The mist drifting. A good day for the resting in the cracks of time.

Just him and not them, and not ever them.

This endless wanting of theirs.

In the valley.

In the garden.

And then?

Nothing, and always betraying that which they said they did know.

With his cigarette dangling from his lips, he jumped from the pickup, and he walked to the front of the garage and pushed open the wooden double doors and stepped into the night.

Don't be denied.

Why would I?

That's right.

Why?

I won't be, and never will be.

Jonathan rode the middle of the dirt road. He stopped and turned in the saddle. He'd searched everywhere, from their place to here. He'd spoken with each of his neighbors, the men there, in their fields, all of them with the same look and tone suggestive of sympathy and futility of which he did view with scorn and anger. This life of uncertainties and broken possibilities rooted in these exchanges, the cause of which he did not know, or care to know. Why would I? Just find her.

And he searched farther yet, the short stretches of timber between the farms, the long stretches of cliffs above the seaway.

He turned back in the saddle, his wrists resting on the pommel. He was less than a mile to the mainland, and he'd hoped to find whoever it was he was looking for, or at least a sign of them, before they reached there. It'd be harder over there, he'd never been to the mainland. He leaned forward and scratched Destiny behind the ear. We'll find em.

He reached the point where the peninsula joined the mainland. It was less than a mile wide with just the one road in and out, and whoever it was he was looking for had to cross there, sooner or later, if they hadn't already. He looked for a place to camp and wait, and he rode toward the tree line where it bent and ran parallel with the mainland road, just beyond a grassy field.

Leonard wedged a screwdriver between the starter posts of the battery, and he tried the truck. It started. He shut it off. He reached for his cigarettes in his shirt pocket. He lit one with a dented silver Zippo lighter and he put the smokes back in his pocket. He flipped the lid of the lighter shut. He opened it again, and shut it again. Over and over. He exhaled, white smoke in the cold night air.

He walked out of the garage and tried the mudroom door. It was locked. He tucked his hand into the sleeve of his canvas coat and punched out the lower right square of glass. He reached through the broken glass to the inside latch and unlocked the door. He flicked his cigarette away and watched the orange heater arc and fall in the bushes next to the door, and he entered the house.

He opened the gun rack, looked inside and closed it. He walked into the kitchen and looked inside the fridge and took out a pitcher of milk and tipped back a long sip. He put it back and wiped his coat sleeve across his mouth. He reached back into the fridge and pulled out a plate of meat covered in clear plastic wrap. He uncovered it and picked out a thick lamb chop. He sniffed it, took a bite, and closed the fridge. With the plate in one hand and the lamb chop in the other, he started to leave the kitchen. He stuck the lamb chop in his mouth and reached over the kitchen table and took two green apples from a white ceramic bowl and put them in his coat pocket. He took the lamb chop from his mouth and walked up the stairs and down the hallway to the end room where he pushed open the door with his foot and entered. He walked to the bed, sat, placed the plate on the table next to Conor's medicine, and leaned back crossing his heavy black boots. He took another bite of the lamb chop and closed his eyes, and he thought, there was no other place he'd want to be, not this day, other than right here, right now, and he felt good about that. He closed his eyes, and he slept.

Jonathan made camp just beyond the open field in a thick stand of tall pine trees next to the two intersecting dirt roads. Across the mainland road, a small gas station with a single pump. There was a metal hooded lamp, suspended from a curved pole, hanging above the entrance. The light flickered. The lot was littered with rusted cars and trucks, used tires, and various broken and rusted appliances. There were islands of tall grass and weeds coming up from the gravel everywhere.

He stripped Destiny down and let her graze the tall grass. The ground and everything around him were wet, and he sat on a fallen log with the saddle and saddlebag spread over the log next to him, the shotgun resting against the log. He reached into the saddlebag and took out the jar of onions. He ate a few and put the jar back and pulled the collar of his Mac around his neck and he looked out to the darkness, and he waited.

Rachael was on her swing. The chain squeaking. She looked at the house. Her father would be in the study, at his desk, sipping whiskey and reading. She might read, too, but she didn't really want to be in the house. Not right now. She looked at the garage. She wanted to cry, but she thought, she cries too much, and so she jumped off the swing and she went for a walk, down the driveway and back again. One lap and then another, over and over. Thinking and wondering. But wondering about what? Other than her mother, wondering about what?

Her father. She wondered about him too.

Worried, she thought, mostly.

And she walked more.

Conor's pickup moved through the intersection and turned right into the gas station lot, stopping next to the lone gas pump.

Leonard got out and walked to the pump and lifted the handle. He squeezed the trigger. The pump was off. He squeezed it again. He looked around, the light of the partial moon upon the road and the heavy dark shape of woods surrounding the road. He looked back at the gas pump and he smashed the nozzle into the glass on the front of the pump.

A dog began to bark.

Jonathan woke and walked to the edge of the field and saw his father's pickup driving away. He hurried and packed up his things and tacked up Destiny. He slipped the gun over his head and mounted up. He kicked Destiny, and he rode across the short field, through the crossroads, and down the gravel road.

I'll build up the fire, and she did, her father watching her from his desk, looking over the top of his reading glasses.

Are you going to read?

Rachael sat in her chair by the fire and reached for her book. Yes, she said, a little. It's good we got the car back.

Yes, it is. Did the woman upset you?

I don't know. Not too much, I guess.

He didn't say anything else, watching his daughter reading, his heart breaking, and all that he held there with him now. He wanted to, but he couldn't say anything more. He found it too hard. Too awkward. Unknowing if it would unsettle her more than she already was, talking of that which was always there between them, slowly becoming part of who they were now. So much unsaid. Both of them becoming less in this horrible breaking loneliness and sadness. And he hated the thought of that, like one hates any weakness, or more, the inability to overcome it. Worse yet, there was more to come, for her, not him, and he couldn't bring himself to speak of that. Not yet. He'd have to soon enough. More sadness in an already sad world with only the sound of a swing to keep it all at bay. What kind of life was that? None, he thought, and he went back to his book, and he read more, and he drank more.

The hand-painted sign above the overhanging porch read, Morningstar General Store. Jonathan tied the horse to the porch rail and walked up the single wooden step onto the dusty worn porch boards and opened the door, a little silver bell at the top right corner of the door catching and ringing.

From somewhere at the back of the store came the soft crackling sounds of Sarah Vaughan singing September Song.

A small fire burned in an open airtight stove in the far front corner of the room, the warmth of the orange flicker reaching him.

Two small Formica tables with turquoise tops and matching chairs. A small side window with faded yellow curtains. An old sagging red couch along the front wall beneath a large window without curtains.

An old man sat on the couch next to the fire reading a book. He had long white hair tucked behind his ears and a white mustache, red swollen ankles sticking out over the sides of scuffed black leather shoes, the thin black laces undone and looped crazy-like through the eyelets.

In the middle of the room, four long shelves running front to back, each filled with various food items, household supplies, hardware, and assorted automobile parts.

A middle-aged plump woman with shoulder-length red hair emerged from behind a blanket strung over a door at the back of the store. She walked behind a long glass display case running most of the length of the left side of the room, one side of it displaying various candies and sweets, the other, meats and cheeses.

Jonathan studied a blackboard menu hanging on the wall behind the counter.

The woman took up an apron from a hook and placed it over her head. What can I get ya?

I'll have breakfast, if I can get one?

Course ya can. She looked behind her. Don't mind that, I haven't changed it over from last night yet. What'ya have?

Eggs over and bacon.

Coffee?

Regular.

Toast?

Yes, please.

Grab yourself a seat, it'll be right up. Hey?

Jonathan, walking to a table, stopped and looked back at the woman.

Are you Conor's boy?

He nodded.

I'm sorry to hear the news.

Thank you.

You look like him.

Jonathan took the gun off and leaned it against the wall. He sat and looked back at the wall above the counter, at the stuffed animal heads, guns and rifles, and animal traps for sale.

You goin huntin?

Jonathan looked at the old man. Sorry?

I said, are you goin huntin?

No, sir, I'm not.

I thought maybe it was wild cats you were goin for, they're in season all year round. That your horse?

Jonathan looked out the window.

It's been some time since anyone rode up here on a horse, I can tell ya that much.

I'm looking for somebody.

Oh?

They took our truck.

Stole it?

Yup.

Well, it is true, there are scoundrels and thieves among us, that's for damn sure. Always has been, always will be.

A red '62 Ford pickup. It would have come by here sometime last night, or maybe early this morning.

Nope, nothing. Maybe Sally seen it?

Seen what? She placed Jonathan's coffee in front of him and from her apron she took out his eating utensils wrapped in a white paper napkin and placed them on the table.

A red '62, is that what you said, boy? '62?

He nodded and took a sip of coffee.

A red '62, what kind did ya say it was?

A Ford.

A red—.

I can hear em just fine, thank you very much. She looked at Jonathan. Sorry, but you're the first customer we've had today. Why? Was it stolen?

He said he thinks it might have been, yup.

She looked out the front window. That your horse?

Jonathan nodded and took another sip of coffee.

Imagine that. Your eggs'll be up in minute. And you, Samuel Stormfield, leave the boy alone and let em eat his breakfast in peace.

He's not bothering me.

He will.

Never mind her, said the old man, she don't know what she's talking about half the time, the other half, she don't really care anyway. Where you from?

New Arcadia.

I been down there, off and on over the years.

The woman looked back before disappearing behind the blanket covering the doorway. He's Conor McLean's boy.

Is that right?

Yes, sir.

A good man. Sorry 'bout the news. I worked down there, when I was just a young man myself. Did some work for a fella, I can't remember his name now? It's a hard enough life though, ain't it?

It's not so bad.

A frog jumped out from the man's suit pocket. Anyone helpin ya look, or is it just you?

Jonathan sipped his coffee. Was that a frog?

I believe it might have been, yes. Nobody else helpin ya?

Just me.

Just you and your mother then? No brothers or sisters?

Nope. Just us. But she's missing.

Your mother?

Yup.

The woman reappeared and placed Jonathan's breakfast plate in front of him.

His father is dead and his mother is missin.

I know his father is, you damn fool, so did you. She looked at Jonathan. Your mother's missing?

He nodded.

When?

Night before last.

Your father's wake?

Yes.

My God, I'm sorry.

You haven't had it so good lately, have ya, boy? said the old man.

You think maybe your mother took the truck?

It was there when she went missing. It was there when I left to find her.

Why didn't you take the truck? asked the woman.

It wasn't running. He broke off a piece of toast and tipped it into his eggs.

But it is now?

I guess it is, cause I saw it come this way last night. It was dark, and I couldn't see who was driving.

Sally lit a cigarette and inhaled. She exhaled and blew out the match. You think whoever took it had something to do with your mom goin missin?

Jonathan finished chewing a mouthful of breakfast and looked at the woman. They were camped out on our place and broke into the house.

What'd they take? asked the old man.

My dad's gun.

Sally flicked her ash in an ashtray on the end table next to the couch and she turned away and raised her head and exhaled. She looked back. That it?

I heard a noise and woke up and they must of left. He finished the last of his eggs. How much do I owe you?

You ate that quick, said the old man.

I'm in a hurry.

Never mind, dear, the till ain't even opened yet.

Are ya sure?

She inhaled. Yeah, I'm sure.

Thank you. He picked up his gun and walked to the door.

You know, the old man said.

Jonathan stopped and looked back.

If it was me, I'd treat this like I was huntin wild cats.

How's that?

Don't give em an even chance, if ya can help it. Good luck, boy.

The little bell on the door jangled, and the screen door slammed shut.

He ain't had it so good lately.

Nope, said the old man, and you can see it too, he's got blood in his eyes.

Leonard was back at the old couples house, the old man's body he'd left on the broken patio stones, dragged and chewed at, with just parts of his head and face left, torn clothes, and other parts unwanted. Unholy creatures of the night, he thought. Bastard wild dogs. Rabid ones, most likely.

He entered the garage and fished out the jerry can he'd seen earlier. There was at least half a can. Maybe more.

He poured the gas into the truck, dropped the can, and walked into the house. He opened the refrigerator door and took out some wrapped up leftover chicken. He sat at the table. He got back up and removed a carton of milk from the refrigerator and sat back down. I wonder how much they did love one another?

He took a sip of milk.

All those years.

He ate some more, and he thought about that.

All that time together. What that must have been like.

63

Love, he thought. Big moon, or not, and then gone.

Just like that.

Jonathan heard a sound and stopped. Metal against rock. He listened. Nothing. He looked. A wall of evergreens, thick underbrush, and young white birch trees. He swung his shotgun around and moved his horse forward and stopped again. He leaned toward the woods. Hello? He turned the horse and rode back to the mouth of the long gravel driveway. He kicked the horse and rode up it.

Holly exhaled. Fuck, she said, and she watched the rider, a morning mug of coffee in her one hand, her heavy chain in the other. She stretched, trying to keep the rider in her sights, her long hair falling over her faded green vinyl winter coat with puffs of synthetic stuffing sticking out from various places. Under her coat she wore a full-length white cotton nightgown with a lace design covering the top of her breasts. Black army boots, scuffed and dirty and scratched, the laces undone, the tongues flopping forward.

The driveway bent to the left and Jonathan stopped. He waited and he listened. He moved forward and a rundown white clapboard house came into view, a broken and slanted wooden deck out front. The left side of the front window boarded up with plywood, the edges and the corners black with mildew.

Through the one good window he saw the furniture pushed to the walls, several men asleep on various chairs and couches, empty liquor bottles on tables, a vacant poker table and chairs in the middle of the room.

He looked for his pickup among the cars and pickups lining the driveway and parked on the lawn. It wasn't there. Beyond the vehicles to the right of the house was a small white and blue camper-trailer. In front of the house, a dead patch of grass and weeds where a heavy chain was staked in the ground by an iron rod. He followed the chain with his eyes to where it disappeared in the woods.

Just a dog, he said, and he turned the horse and started back down the driveway.

Holly watched the rider returning, and start back up the road.

Should she call to him? Should she?

She wanted to.

Was he safe?

She leaned forward watching the rider until he dropped from her view. Longer yet, and a tear came. She rubbed it away. What good would that do? She got up and walked away on the well-worn path through the woods holding the chain over her arm like she would the train of some long dress.

She walked across the dead grass to the trailer at the side of the house, and she climbed the metal stair and stopped and looked at the slanted garage and a jacked-up Chevy pickup. There was a rusted toolbox next to it with tools laid out on a grease-stained canvas drop sheet and a disposable propane torch. She looked at the house, and she walked back down the stair.

She gathered the chain in her arms and walked toward the torch letting the chain out as she went. She reached the front bumper of the truck and the chain ran out. She dropped to her knees and stretched out, there were still several feet of space between her and the torch.

She got back up onto her knees she looked around. She stood and walked toward the woods and found a tall branch and snapped the tip off. She walked to her right, keeping the chain tight as she went. She stretched out again and extended the branch forward and swung it as hard as she could, knocking the torch forward. She got up and walked toward the bumper and stretched out again and reached for it. Using the stick, she knocked it toward her.

She dropped the branch and picked up the torch and walked to the back of the trailer. She stopped and picked up a large rock and brought it with her. She set the rock on the ground next to her and reached into her coat pocket and pulled out her smokes. She opened the pack and tipped out a small disposal lighter. She squatted and straightened the chain out close to her ankle. She turned the black valve knob and when she heard it hiss, she flicked her lighter on and held it to the end of the burn tube. The torch starting startled her. She looked back at the house. She held the flame to a section of the chain and when the metal began to glow orange, she placed the torch to the side and picked up the rock and smashed it down onto the chain. It didn't break. She did it again and it remained intact. She dropped the rock and held the flame back to the chain. The torch sputtered, hissed, and dropped out. She placed the torch on the ground and picked up the rock with both hands and raised it above her head. She drove it down as hard as she could onto the chain, and it broke.

Jonathan came to a narrow dirt road that ran north and he stopped and looked. He turned back and saw a woman riding a bicycle pulling a large wooden cart. She rode toward him, stopping at the side of the road.

She was an old woman with wiry gray hair sticking out at different angles from a red satin scarf. She set the kickstand and walked to the side of the cart and lifted open a side panel door. She reached for a looped piece of twine nailed to the roof and hooked it over a nail at the top of the panel. She removed two wooden yellow stools from the cart and set them on the road. She flopped down a hinged tabletop with a hinged wooden leg. She looked at Jonathan. Get off that damn horse and have a seat.

She unfurled a black cloth over the table and laid out the instruments of her trade: tarot cards, a wooden cup filled with bones, a mason jar filled with tea, a crystal ball, a cup and saucer. Which?

Which what?

She pointed to each one. Tarot cards, bones, tea leaves, which?

Have you seen a red pickup?

It'll cost ya extra, but I can check.

I meant driving by.

I ain't seen nobody or anything in more than three days, you're the first, and so far, you ain't workin out so good. Now which?

He nodded toward the road running north. What about up there?

She closed her eyes and sighed. Fine. She opened her eyes. I'll read your palm.

Well?

There's nothing up there, that's what. Not a good goddamn thing. Now hold your hand out.

I don't want my future told.

What'ya mean, you don't want your future told? Who in their right mind doesn't wanna know what the world holds in store for em? Everybody does. Now come on, get off that horse and let's cheat that two-faced bitch of God's lust.

Who?

Fate, boy, God's own mistress. Besides, you might just find out you're about to inherit a million dollars and marry a pin-up girl. What'ya think about that?

He looked at the road stretching out before him. What's down there?

There's nothing down there, that's what. Nothin but trouble and pain. Now lean over.

Sorry?

If you don't want your future told, I'll tell you a story.

A story?

I know plenty.

No, thank you.

Seen it all and lived to tell about it. She stepped closer. Look, you're just a boy, what do you know? And soon you'll be a man and know even less. Now close your eyes.

Close my eyes?

She leaned her hands against the horse and stood on her toes and whispered, close your eyes and I'll talk dirty to ya. It'll cost ya a little extra, but it'll be worth it, you'll see.

I'm in a hurry.

Of course, you're in a hurry.

I gotta go.

Well, that's just fine, ain't it then? But you remember this, time gone is time here again, and it multiplies. And that's the truth of it. She fell back to the flats of her feet and walked to her cart, talking to herself, muttering as she went, what's the damn rush, hurrin about and doin what? Runnin in circles, over and over. For what purpose? If ya listened to me, you'd be far better off. She looked back at Jonathan. I know what I know, boy, I read the signs, and I'll tell you what, yours is not a good sign on account of your wantin too much. Did ya hear me? All the time wantin too much. You think about that.

Jonathan rode on looking back at the woman packing up her things, closing the side panel of the cart.

She looked back at Jonathan and yelled, dirty stories, boy. Everybody wants dirty stories.

He rode past the side road running north.

Holly, in the distance, walked from the woods lining the road. She stopped, looked south, and turned and ran north.

Crows were picking at decayed bug-infested meat clinging to the bleached bones of some past life.

Jonathan stopped and watched.

What's your name, son?

He looked and saw a woman with her head sticking out past a row of small twisted scrub pines. He rode up to her, the crows jumping and crying out, and flying away.

She was sitting on a stump next to a narrow driveway that disappeared amongst the trees, the bottom half of her pants caked with blood.

The crows came back, settling on the road and picking again at the bones.

Well?

Well what?

What's your name?

Jonathan.

Unhuh. Where you from, Jonathan?

New Arcadia.

The woman leaned to her side and let a long spit of tobacco juice slide from her mouth. Pleased to meet ya. I'm Jackie, from Carlsbad.

This is Carlsbad?

Nope. This is nowhere.

You're bleeding.

Bad veins. It's been a heavy load. All my life. But don't think I wasn't a hard-ass, despite it all, because I was. Damn right, I was. But there comes a point, that's all, and she leaned to the side again and let another long spill of tobacco juice fall.

A tippin point. A person can only take so much, ya know, before they start thinkin all sorts of crazy things, and then the next thing you know, you're sittin by the side of the road, bleedin out, afraid of the dark, wonderin, all the time wonderin. Seeing shadows. Seeing em everywhere. And by God are they. She leaned forward. It can happen when you get to be my age. You remember that. A damn tragic, and horrible thing. But what's to be done of it, that's the question.

Have ya seen a red pickup?

The woman leaned back. I see everything that comes up or down this road, less of course it comes at night, then I got no interest in it. No, sir, none at all. Come dark, I relinquish this seat to the night dwellers.

Night dwellers?

Evil doers. Propagators of darkness. There ain't a soul alive, who, if they got somethin good to contribute, can't contribute it during daylight hours. The same cannot be said about those whose contributions can only be made during the night.

This pickup, it was red. A '62 Ford.

I ain't seen it. Not today I ain't.

What about yesterday?

Nope, not then neither. She leaned forward and spat again. Why ya askin?

Someone stole it.

Is that right?

You see a woman on a bike pulling a cart?

Robin Walker's Amazing Fortune-Telling for Hire?

Yeah, that one.

You're not much of a trustin type, are ya?

He didn't answer.

No? Well, I'd suggest you find out, that is if you're planning on havin any sort of say in how you live your life. And if you're smart, you'll get yourself off this road by dark.

A black '69 Impala drove by and stopped, spooking Destiny. Jonathan reining her in.

The heavy Chevy engine rumbled, the dust settling. A man squinting his eyes looked back at them from the rear-view mirror.

Jonathan and the woman watched to see what would happen next.

The car remained idling, and finally, the man drove off.

See what I mean? said the woman.

It's not dark yet.

No, but it's comin.

Jonathan turned Destiny and nodded back at the woman. Thanks, anyway.

Son?

Jonathan stopped.

Listen to me, I know what I know, and in the night, evil begets evil, and that's the truth of it. It accumulates and has since the beginning of time. And keep in mind, too, it knows no alliance, not even to its own self, especially its own self. Be careful out there, that's all I'm saying, and she leaned forward and spat again.

Thank you, I will, and he kicked the horse and rode down the road.

He lit a smoke and leaned his elbow on the open window frame of the pickup truck. He smoked, and he watched a car approaching. He looked down at the Colt .45 on the bench seat next to him and picked it up and placed it on his lap.

The Impala made the turn onto the driveway and stopped next to the pickup, Rooke leaning over and putting down the passenger window. Ya seen a girl walkin around?

Leonard looked at the man, his pale pink skin, green eyes, greasy long fair hair tucked behind his ears, the small broken blood vessels scattered across his nose. What girl?

Have ya seen one or not?

It's hard to say if I don't know which one.

She's got long brown hair and could be draggin around part of a chain.

A chain?

That's what I said. Did ya see her or not?

Well, I don't know.

Rooke picked up a Beretta semiautomatic and pointed it at Leonard through the open window.

Leonard smiled. The only one I seen today was older and she wasn't draggin a chain.

Rooke put the gun back on the seat next to him. Asshole, he said, and he backed the car up and headed down the road.

Holly stayed to the ditch, walking and dragging the short length of chain through the tall grass and weeds, her green vinyl coat tied around her waist, her white cotton nightgown bunched up beneath her coat and falling just past her knees. She was tired, her face flushed from walking and trying to run, while having to constantly watch out in all directions. Her feet were sore in her laced boots, and she was thirsty. She looked at the ankle bracelet, the raw skin around it.

She walked more, despite the pain.

She stopped again and looked around. She knew she couldn't stay on the road. But where? There was nothing but ditches and fields and the odd tree. She took to the deep ditch and the tall grass, and she kept walking.

Rachael's father looked over the top of his glasses and said, would you like to play the Alice game?

Rachael looked up from her book and nodded and smiled and said yes.

Would you tell me, please, which way I ought to go from here? said her father.

Rachael said, *That depends a good deal on where you want to get to, said the Cat.*

Her father said, *I don't much care where, said Alice.*

And Rachael said, *Then it doesn't matter which way you go, said the Cat.*

Her father said, *So long as I get somewhere, said Alice.*

Oh, you're sure to do that, if you only walk long enough, said the Cat. Do another one, said Rachael.

Hold on, let me look in the book, these are getting too easy for you.

Rachael smiled.

Here we go. *Against Idleness and Mischief. How doth the little busy bee—.*

Improve each shining hour, said Rachael.

Very good, said her father. *And gather honey all the day.*

From every opening flower! said Rachael.

In books, or work, or healthful play, said her father.

Let my first years be passed, said Rachael.

That I may give for every day, said her father.

Some good account at last. Said Rachael.

Well done. Why don't I give you a hand with supper? So, I myself might give a good account at last. At least this day.

That's okay, you don't have to.

No, I'd like to.

Are you sure?

What are we making? Let me guess. He stood, his hand moving quickly to his desk to steady himself. Pasta?

And corn.

Oh good. Lead the way.

He waited for Rachael, and he followed, doing his best to steady his walk.

Car lights shone in the woods, and Jonathan reached for his shotgun. He heard a car door open and close. He stood and listened, and he walked forward.

Evenin.

Jonathan turned and looked behind him at the tall thin man from the Impala moving toward the small fire.

There's no need for a gun. The man squatted next to the fire and warmed his hands. I'm Rooke Johnson.

Jonathan walked to the fire.

Ya wouldn't have a drink you could offer a man, would ya?

No.

What about to smoke? Ya got any of those? The man stood and reached into his front pant pocket and pulled out a crumpled cigarette pack. He was one-and-done, and he threw the empty pack onto the fire. He squatted and lifted a stick from the fire and lit the cigarette, and he threw the stick back. You don't have much of an outfit here, do ya?

I'm all right.

Is that right? He took a drag of his cigarette and he studied Jonathan. I don't believe I know you, do I, boy?

No.

Rooke looked at Destiny. He looked back at Jonathan. You're the one I saw on the road.

Jonathan didn't answer.

Where ya from?

New Acadia. Why, you ever been there?

Me? Why would I do that? There's nothin down there but a bunch of backward ass farmers. What is it you're doin up this way?

Not much.

Not much?

No.

Rooke leaned forward and spat onto the fire. I'm looking for somebody.

Oh?

My daughter. She's run off.

Your daughter?

In a kind-of-a way, yeah.

I haven't seen her.

How do you know if you ain't seen her or not if you don't know what she looks like?

I've only seen one, and she was older than you.

The man stood and reached into his back pocket and pulled out a pint of whiskey. He held it before him, there was less than two fingers left in the bottle. He gave it a shake and unscrewed the top and finished it. He screwed the top back on and threw the empty bottle into the woods. Well, I'll tell ya what, farmer-boy, if you come across that little slut of mine, you can tell her for me, I'll find her, no matter where she goes. He walked past Jonathan and through the thin line of woods toward the road.

What's she look like?

The man stopped and looked back, backlit by the car's headlights. What's she look like? She's seventeen and no fuckin good, that's what she looks like.

He watched the man leave, and he listened to the Impala pulling away. He unhooked the wineskin from the saddlebag and walked to Destiny. He unscrewed the cap and poured water into his cupped hand and held it out to her. It's a strange place, isn't it? She finished the water and moved her nose to the wineskin and snorted. Yeah, hold on. He filled his hand again, and she drank more.

He rolled his blanket out next to the fire and lifted the saddle and saddlebag onto it. He leaned the shotgun against the saddle and sat down. He looked through the saddlebag for the jerky and pickled eggs, and he began to eat.

A drifting mist diffused the early morning light, Jonathan riding the road. He came to a long driveway. He stopped. The unknown, and the quiet, amongst the mist making him pause. He dismounted and lead Destiny by the reins up the driveway. A stucco house came into view, and he stopped. He walked a little more and stopped again. He looked at the open garage door. He looked toward the house. He walked forward and saw what was left of the old man. He dropped the reins and unsnapped the shotgun strap. He looked back down at what was just the stain of a person. Dried dark pooled blood on broken patio stones. He looked at the screen door and the kitchen beyond the door. He climbed the stairs and looked closer. Hello? He opened the door and walked inside.

There was a mug of coffee on the kitchen table.

He walked through the house, the gun at its ready, calling out.

It was quiet. The house empty.

He walked up the stairs, and he walked to the open bedroom door. He entered the room, and he saw the old woman on the floor, and he walked up to her. He saw her freed finger next to her, and he looked away, out the window, to the distant tree line beyond the garage and the long distance it traveled back from there, and he said, Jesus Christ.

The brightness of the sun washed out her father, a tall man dressed in a three-piece suit wearing a white apron and standing on the dusty wooden porch of their store. He reached into a bushel basket of red apples and held one out in front of himself, the sun reflecting off the newness of the apple.

Holly, just a young girl in a dress, barefoot on the porch boards, reached up to it.

And he was there now, squatting before her, looking at her shackled ankle, at the red welts and bruising, the thin lines of dried blood running to her foot. He looked at Holly, and he said, it doesn't look so good.

She retracted her foot and tried to hide it beneath her other leg.

Have you tried picking the lock?

She nodded her head.

No luck, huh? He reached up to the wide silk band around his straw fedora and removed a long pin.

You've been gone a long time.

I know, baby girl. Does it hurt?

A little.

He reached into his pocket and pulled out an apple. Here ya go.

Thanks, Daddie.

You're welcome. All right, hold your leg still.

She bit into the apple and watched her father pick the lock, the shackle separating. Oh my God, she said, and she leaned forward and ran her hand over her ankle. How'd you do that?

She looked up and saw her father climbing the ten-strand wire fence that edged the ditch, the ankle bracelet and chain hanging over his shoulder. He looked back. It's an older model and it wasn't really that difficult at all.

Where are you going now? And she watched him fading into the sunlight, the sound of the trap and the chain rattling over his shoulder.

Daddie?

Rooke pulled up and stopped at the side of the road, the Impala idling. He got out and walked around the car, down the deep ditch, and up again, and held the gun to Holly's forehead. Get the fuck up.

She opened her eyes.

Jonathan was back in the kitchen. He walked to a wall mounted yellow rotary phone and picked up the receiver. There was no dial tone. He hung it up, and he looked around.

He walked outside and stood over what was left of the old man. And he wondered again, what kind of place this was. He didn't know. None he wanted to be a part of, that was for damn sure.

He looked for Destiny, and seeing her at the side of the garage grazing the tall grass there, he walked to her, picked up the reins, and started to walk back up the driveway.

Rachael finished cleaning up the breakfast dishes and walked out the backdoor, and stood on the small back porch. She looked at the day. She looked at the garage, and she walked to her swing. She sat on it, and she pushed herself with her foot, slowly, back and forth. A low squeak coming from the chains. She was waiting. That's what it felt like. But for what? She looked at the house, and she wanted her father to walk out the door and smile and say, need a push? Sometimes he did. Not lately, though. And they would chat. It didn't have to be about her. That'd be okay if it wasn't. But she wished he would. She pushed off the ground with her foot harder and she got the swing going faster, pumping her legs, the chains squeaking louder, and she got the swing going high as she could, and higher yet, higher than all the world—for that's what she wanted. That way, she thought, she wouldn't be standing still all the time, waiting.

Isn't that right, Alice?

One day.

What she hoped for.

She pumped her legs harder.

That which she wished for, every day.

Hey.

Jonathan stopped and looked.

Ya want some lunch?

He was unsure if the woman in the field was speaking to him. He looked around to see if there was anyone else.

The woman laughed. Ya, you. Who else would I be talkin to? C'mon, I got plenty.

Jonathan sat the horse.

I won't bite. I promise.

He rode down and up the wide ditch and onto to the grassy field. He stopped and looked at the woman. She had long, thick, auburn hair and freckles. She was wearing a long print summer dress over white thermal long johns, thick gray socks pulled up past her brown leather hiking boots. Over the top of the dress she wore a thick gray sweater. Hanging from a wide brown leather belt were a half dozen snake skins. She held a hunting knife with a wide blade.

I like your horse.

Thanks.

What's her name?

Destiny.

Destiny?

Yeah.

That's a nice name.

Thanks.

Well, c'mon down, lunch is just about ready.

Jonathan dismounted and wrapped the reins around the pommel of the saddle and backed the girth strap off and let the horse graze the tall field grass.

The woman pointed her knife toward the blanket spread out on the grass next to a campfire where something was cooking in a small cast-iron frying pan. Have a seat. On the blanket was a sawed-off shotgun, a pair of binoculars, a bottle of wine, a wine glass, and a plate. Goodness me, where are my manners. My name's Priscilla, although my daddie always called me, Miss Lady Feryl, but Priscilla's fine.

He shook her hand. Jonathan.

Pleased to meet you, Jonathan. Have a seat.

He took his shotgun off and he sat and placed the gun on the blanket.

Priscilla squatted next to the fire and tended to the cooking strips of meat, onions, and peppers. Here, have a glass of wine. It's French. She poured a glass and handed it to him. Here's to company, and she held up the bottle.

They each took a sip.

So why did you, anyway? asked Jonathan.

Why'd I what? Invite ya to lunch?

Yeah.

I dunno, I had my glasses on ya. She nodded toward the binoculars. And ya seemed nice enough. Besides, I'm celebratin and felt like some company, and there you were, just like that, plain as day, riding a horse. And I can tell ya what, it's not every day you see that, now is it?

What are you celebrating?

Today's my last day on the job. She used her hunting knife to mix the food in the frying pan. That's getting a little too hot, and she set the frying pan on the edge of the fire.

Doing what?

Huntin snakes, of course.

Snakes?

Yup. She shook the skins attached to her belt. They're worth a fortune.

Snake skins?

Oh yeah, they use em for lots of things, boots, wallets, purses, you name it. Especially these big black rat snakes. She shook a couple of the large black and copper skins. They grow big, which is good, up to five or six feet, even bigger, if ya get lucky. She grabbed the cloth next to the fire and picked up the frying pan and scooped out a portion onto the plate. She put the pan back on the edge of the fire and passed the plate to Jonathan.

Thanks.

My pleasure. You got your own knife, I suppose.

Jonathan unsheathed his knife and scooped a mouthful.

Makes a nice little meal, don't it?

Jonathan stopped chewing and pointed his knife at the snake skins hanging from her belt.

Priscilla laughed. What'ya think it was? Chicken?

Jonathan swallowed the food and took a sip of wine.

She smiled. You're somethin, I dunno what, but you're definitely somethin. I could set ya up in business, if ya wanted to. I'm quittin anyway. What'ya say? Ya interested?

Thanks, but we have a farm.

Oh? Where's that?

New Acadia.

Would you look at that, I don't even know where that is. Am I not the most ignorant thing you ever met? But I'm sure it's nice. What kind of farm is it?

Mostly sheep.

Too bad. You can make a killin doin this.

So why you quitting?

I'm goin to Paris, France.

Paris, France?

Yup. I'm gonna travel. See some civilization. I deserve it after huntin snakes in these God forsaken woods for the last ten years. Hell, there ain't been a single day I haven't thought about it. Over and over, like a broken record. And now I'm goin. I got pretty much every dollar I ever made chasin these limbless little bastards, and it ain't a day too soon, neither, I can tell ya that much. I was goin crazy, certifiable, lock me up crazy. Worse than that, I'd of killed somebody, maybe even my own self. I kid you not. A person can only take so many days livin with an itch they can't scratch. You know what I mean? Probably ya don't, but ya can trust me on that. I know all about itches, more than I ever thought I'd wanna know, that's for damn sure. There's types of itches ya can't scratch that will slowly drive you crazy, and I do mean the worse kinda crazy, silent and nuttier than hell in your head type crazy, the kind that builds and builds and won't stop buildin until the next thing ya know you're chasin butterflies through a fire. And then there's the kind you can scratch, but of course, those are the ones you don't wanna have to scratch, least ways, not by your own self. Funny how life works that way, ain't it? Here, have some more wine and let's forget about our troubles. She filled his glass and took another sip from the bottle.

Do you have any family that could take over your work?

Nope, my father died when I was just young. I didn't know my mom. I had a husband, once, but he's dead now too.

I'm sorry.

Don't be, it was some time ago. Besides, he was nothin but a snake in the grass himself. My husband that is. My father was a prince of a man. What about you?

There's just me and my mom, but she's missing.

Oh? I'm sorry to hear that. Is that what you doin, lookin for her?

Jonathan nodded and took another sip.

How come you're riding a horse?

Our truck was stolen.

Someone stole your truck?

Yup.

When did it go missin, the same time as your mom?

Nope, afterwards.

So, your mom went missin, then your truck went missin?

Yeah, and he took another sip of wine.

D'ya think someone did something to her, then took the truck?

I think so.

Well, I hope you find her, Jonathan, I really do. And I hope she's all right.

Thanks.

She topped up Jonathan's glass and tipped back the bottle. She put the bottle down and picked up Jonathan's plate and put it in the frying pan and stood. Finish your wine and relax, I'm just gonna give these a quick rinse in the river down there.

I can help, and he started to stand.

No, that's all right. It'll just take a minute. Sit and enjoy the sunshine. Lord knows we don't get much of it, do we? She began to leave. She stopped and looked back. Ya think ya might've been better off trying to find her first? That way you'd know what happened?

I thought about it, but by then it would've been too late, and they'd be gone.

She looked as if she might say something more but didn't. I'll be right back.

Destiny lifted her head and watched Priscilla walking by.

Jonathan stretched out on the blanket, taking the warmth of the sun to his face, and he closed his eyes.

He opened his eyes and saw Priscilla standing before him.

I changed my mind. She placed the dishes on the ground and sat and unlaced her boots.

Jonathan sat up.

Why should I waste all that fine wine and this lovely sunshine doin dishes? She slipped her boots and socks off and stood and pulled her heavy sweater over her head. She undid her belt with the snake skins hanging from it and dropped it to the ground. She pulled her dress over her head and stood in her small pair of white panties, a silver chain with a silver snake head hanging around her neck. I told ya I was celebratin, didn't I? What are ya waitin for? Take your coat off.

Jonathan didn't move, just staring at Priscilla.

She laughed, walked forward, and straddled his lap. Here, let me help ya.

She took his coat off, and undid his shirt. She undid his belt, and she pushed him onto his back—desire. All of it. The cold loneliness of unfulfillment seeking the scent and strength of his young body.

Jonathan succumbing to the flooding of pleasure—an objective first fuck of what is this?

Leonard drove by and saw Destiny grazing in the field, and he slowed the pickup. He saw Jonathan stretched out sleeping, and he took his foot off the brake and drifted forward. He turned right up the narrow dirt road.

He drove slowly, trying to look past a long line of ash trees. He came to an opening and saw Priscilla walking across the field carrying the dirty dishes. He crossed over a small wooden bridge and pulled into a clearing cut in the thick woods just past the bridge. He parked in the upper left side of the clearing and got out. It was warm, and he took his coat off and threw it in the truck. He closed the door quietly, and he walked to the bottom edge of the clearing.

Priscilla came upon the embankment above the river. She approached the soft bank and looked toward the bridge where a strong current flowed. She walked there and knelt down and began to rinse the frying pan, dishes, and wine glass.

She was done, and she leaned over the water and cupped her hands to take a drink. Leonard, reaching out from the shadows beneath the bridge, pushed her head under the water and held it there.

She struggled, her arms stiff and straight behind her, her hands making small circles clutching the air behind her. She kicked her left leg out and Leonard smiled. He knelt and began to lift her head and turn it toward him. He leaned over the water so she could see him, and she fought harder. She couldn't hold her breath any longer and bubbles began to escape her mouth. More came. A steady stream. He watched with interest, Priscilla opening her mouth and gasping for air and taking in water.

He lifted her head and cupped his left hand over her mouth, and he dragged her to her feet, limp in his arms, sucking in air through her nose. She began to gag. He spread his fingers and she vomited, mostly brownish water.

She tried to kick again, a weak kick that found his shin. He took his knife from his pocket and flipped it open. Her eyes flared, and she began to struggle more.

He put the knife to her throat and moved his mouth next to her ear. I see you've met my friend?

She began to struggle again, and he held her tighter. She bit his hand and she kicked his shin.

Goddamn it. I'll put an end to this right now, if you keep that up.

She began to cry.

There we go. That's better. We don't want to disturb little sleeping beauty back there now do we? He looked in the direction of Jonathan. This'll be more fun, with just the two of us.

Jonathan woke. Darkness had begun to fall. He looked and saw Destiny on her side in the tall grass. He picked up his shotgun and walked toward her. He stopped. There was a massive amount of blood surrounding her, the grass soaked with it, her throat stabbed and hacked at and slashed.

He ran to the river.

At the bottom of the slope, he stopped. Priscilla was there, splayed out at an odd angle on her back. He walked along the soft edge of the river stopping several feet before her. Her head was tilted to the side, her eyes looking up, the front of her dress torn away exposing her white freckled breasts. Her right leg broken and folded back, her thermal long underwear cut away and hanging from her legs. There was a pool of blood formed on the grass between her legs where her own knife protruded from her.

He looked up. Who the fuck are you?

The one side of the saddlebag, facing up from the fallen horse, had been emptied, the food taken. He untied the saddlebag strings from the saddle and sat on the ground and placed his feet against Destiny, and he began to push with his legs, wedging the bag back and forth until it became free from beneath her. He checked inside. His change of clothes, money, the compass, and the box of matches were still there.

He took his knife out and cut a slit through the bottom rim on each side of the saddlebag. He cut free the saddle strings and pushed the ends through the cuts he'd made and tied them off. He stood and placed the bag over his shoulder. He picked up his shotgun, and he looked again at Destiny. And he thought, who could do such thing? What kind of person does that?

He approached Priscilla and dropped his shotgun and the saddlebag, and he knelt next to her. He closed her eyes. He looked at her exposed breasts and tried to cover them with her torn sweater. He looked between her legs, at her knife protruding from her. He took hold of the knife, looked away, and he pulled it out. He cleaned the blood from the blade on the grass and put it in his saddlebag.

He stood and sighted for a while the coming darkness. He looked back at Priscilla. Dead in this field. And he thought of his mother.

He picked up his things and placed the saddlebag and shotgun straps over his head. He picked up Priscilla, and put her over his shoulder, and he began to walk.

Holly was stretched across her small bed, asleep now, the blankets skewed beneath her, her nightgown balled up around her neck. Visible on her back were a half-dozen fresh cuts and welts, some still bleeding, piled on top of a crisscrossing of old raised scars from past beatings.

Across from the bed was a small counter with a small sink, a hot plate, and a brown bar fridge. Above the sink, between two brown cupboards, the window was boarded-up, the words, life is good, written in red lipstick. A broken blue plate, a pink plastic cup, and a green broken glass vase were scattered on the floor.

Rachael's father was stretched out on the couch—passed out, and she covered him with the blanket. She raised his head and put a pillow there.

She walked to the fireplace and built the fire up. She climbed onto her chair and pulled her blanket over her. She picked up her book, and instead of reading, she thought, she'd rather talk to Alice. And she said, *I can get big, too, and I can get small, too,* but I don't have a key to a door to fit there. But one day I might. And she thought, but how will I know what door? Or what garden? She looked at the fire. Or where to find it?

Alice?

Down, down, down, said Rachael. *Would the fall never come to an end?*

I wonder how many miles I've fallen this time? I shall fall right ... no, wait. *I wonder if I shall fall right through the earth! Down, down, down.* Was she at the center of the earth too? She didn't know. *Dinah'll miss me very much tonight, I should think! I hope they'll remember her saucer of milk at teatime. Dinah my dear! I wish you were here with me! There are no mice in the air, I'm afraid, but you might catch a bat, and that's very like a mouse, you know. But do cats eat bats, I wonder? And now I'm getting rather sleepy,* yes and me too, *in a dreamy sort of way, Do cats eat bats? Do cats eat bats? and sometimes, Do bats eat cats? for you see, as I couldn't answer either question, it didn't much matter which way I put it.* And now I wonder if I've dozed off, and maybe I have, and I've begun to dream that I am *walking hand in hand with Dinah, and saying to her very earnestly, Now, Dinah, tell me the truth: did you ever eat a bat? when suddenly, thump! thump!*

down I came upon a heap of sticks and dry leaves, and the fall was over, and I was there now, once again, there and running, to the sunshine, in the silence, and yelling, Momma? And I wait and wait and wait and wait more, at the bottom of the hole. And I say, where are you? And there's never any answer, and so I run, and I run more, and I am there, waiting, for you now. For I am Alice.

You're Alice?

Yes, Alice.

No, Rachael. You're Rachael. And always remember, Rachael the Reminder.

Yes.

Yes.

You won't forget.

No, I won't forget.

Ever?

No, not ever.

And she slept more.

Jonathan walked the side of a dirt road carrying Priscilla. He stopped and rested and shifted her weight on his shoulder. He walked again and soon he came upon a faint yellow light coming from a wooded area beyond an open field. Rather than following the road and looking for a driveway, he cut across the field.

The going was hard, and the darkness in the field felt good. Like a shelter from everything that had happened. Everything that could still possibly happen. He wished he hadn't taken the time to have stopped, and wondered what would have happened if he hadn't? Destiny wouldn't be butchered and dead in a field and most likely neither would you, he said to Priscilla, dead weighted on his shoulder.

And what if I hadn't fallen asleep? You might both be alive. And why am I? He didn't know. He continued walking, and he thought, I'll find you, and when I do, I'll kill you.

He came to a line of tall trees, the driveway to the house just beyond them. Two large Chesapeake dogs appeared running toward him from the back of the house. They stopped and showed their teeth, growling, their thick chests heaving in and out. The light in the window of the small log cabin went out. He looked at the dogs, and he swung the shotgun around and pointed it at them.

He walked forward, the dogs snapping and growling and backing up and circling. On the ground was a scattering of bones, the forelegs of deer with their hooves still attached.

The cabin door opened. Whoever you are, you can stop right there.

Call your dogs off. I'm carrying a girl and she's heavy.

What girl?

Her name's Priscilla.

Is she all right?

No, she's not. She's dead.

The man paused. Bring her up. The dogs won't hurt you.

An older Black man, with tight gray curly hair and a broad chubby face, met Jonathan at the door, a shotgun in his hand.

He looked at Pricilla. Dear God Almighty, and he stared at her, lifeless in Jonathan's arms. Come in, he said.

Jonathan followed the man inside the small dark cabin, and the man closed the door. Put her on the table.

He did, her legs dangling over the edge of the table.

What happened?

Jonathan looked over the one room cabin. To the left of the little kitchen area was a double sized brass bed covered with a white lace canopy. A small bedside table with a hurricane lamp turned down low, and a straight back chair next to the bed. He thought there might be someone in the bed. Across the room facing back toward the bed was a large wooden desk and a chair, the desk covered with books and stacks of paper and an old typewriter and another hurricane lamp. Stacked on either side of the desk were tall piles of books.

Son?

Jonathan looked at the man.

What happened?

I don't know.

Where'd you find her?

A couple of miles from here. By a river.

At the base of a field?

Jonathan nodded.

She lived close to there.

You knew her?

Yes, came a woman's voice from the bed.

Jonathan looked in the direction of the voice.

She was like a daughter to us, said the woman. Her family died when she was just young. Come over here.

Jonathan looked at the man.

The man nodded toward the bed, and Jonathan walked to it.

The man looked back at Priscilla. My sweet baby girl, he said, what have they done?

Have a seat, said the woman.

Jonathan remained standing, looking at the bed trying to see who was in there. We need to call the police, he said, and he heard the man's throaty laugh behind him, and he turned back and looked.

There is no phone, son, said the man. Even if there was, what good would it do?

She's with God now, said the woman. You didn't know her?

I only met her today, and Jonathan sat and leaned his shotgun against the bedside table. She said she was going to France.

Yes, that was her dream, said the woman. To travel and see the world, and she would have loved it. She was far too big a soul to remain here. Turn the light up.

Jonathan turned the light up halfway, enough to see the old woman, her face craggy and welled with raised lumps of past lesions, her nose flattened, her fingers shortened and grossly deformed.

I have Hansen's disease. You can look as long as you like. Charles, bring my pipe. Her eyes followed the man walking toward a tall cabinet. She watched him open the doors. She looked back at Jonathan. A long time ago, we did some work together in Burma, for a children's organization. Ten years later, it manifested itself. It's a shame you didn't get to know our little baby girl better. She was an angel, a perfect angel, and the world is now far less of a place than it was—and yet, all the greater for her having been here. I don't know what we'll ever do without her.

The man opened the canopy and sat on the edge of the bed, the woman's opium pipe and bowl laid out on a wooden tray he cradled on his lap.

Thank you, Charles. There's matches in the drawer, son. Light one.

Jonathan pulled the matches from the drawer and struck one.

Light it here, and she pointed.

He held the match to the gas lamp where she indicated, and it caught fire. Charles placed the bowl onto the chimney of the lamp and moved the tray closer to his wife.

She turned her head, her watery eyes searching Jonathan's face for something she'd not seen, that she'd missed, something not right. You're young enough to feel a rage against this, aren't you?

Aren't you?

Rage? No. That would imply my first having to be surprised, then foolish enough to ask why? Saddened, yes. Ever so much.

Charles leaned forward and placed the pipe in his wife's gnarled fingers.

She leaned back, her head resting against a piling of pillows, and she lifted her dream stick and prepared to chase the dragon. She closed her eyes, and she put the pipe to her wet lips and inhaled. She held the smoke in her lungs, her eyes still closed. The man watched Jonathan watching the woman.

She exhaled, a slow steady stream of sweet pungent smoke. She rolled her head and looked at Jonathan. And you? You're chasing other demons, aren't you?

Me?

Yes, you. What are they?

Jonathan paused, the heavy blue opium smoke surrounding him. The same person that did that, he looked at Priscilla, might have done something to my mother.

But you're not sure? She closed her eyes and inhaled again.

No. She went missing the night of my father's wake.

She exhaled. And why do you think this person, who did these horrific things to our baby girl Priscilla, had something to do with that?

Someone broke into our house, and the next day she was gone. I was looking for them when I met Priscilla.

She looked at Jonathan. Come closer.

Jonathan narrowed his eyes and didn't move.

What's your name?

Jonathan.

Jonathan, what I have, you can't catch, do you understand? You need to trust me. And to do that, you must have faith in yourself. You've been judging me since you sat down, have you not? The very same way I've been judging you. It's the reason Charles here hasn't shot you yet. You come here carrying our beautiful Priscilla, butchered, saying you found her like that. Yet we've never seen you before. You have her knife sticking out of your saddlebag, a saddlebag, but no horse. You're not from here, otherwise, you'd have known calling the police would be worse than not calling the police. But I'm trusting you didn't do it because I have faith in myself, not you. I know what the truth is when I see it, and when I hear it. And I know what it isn't. Now come closer.

Jonathan looked at the man sitting on the edge of the bed, in the shadows, giving back nothing. He looked again at the woman, and he leaned forward, the smell of the opium growing stronger.

The woman lifted the pipe to her mouth and inhaled. She held the smoke. She leaned toward Jonathan and exhaled a steady stream of smoke into his waiting mouth. Close your eyes.

He did.

Remember this, Jonathan, the souls of the righteous are in the hands of God, and there shall no torment touch them. In the sight of the unwise they appear to die and their departure is taken for misery, and their going from us to be utter destruction, but they are in peace. Heavenly beautiful peace. May God have mercy.

Jonathan stood at the open door, his saddlebag and shotgun strapped to his back. You're welcome to stay the night here, if you like?

He looked at Priscilla dead on the table. He looked at the woman, sleeping. He looked back at the man. No, thank you. I've lost most of this day as it is. You'll be all right, taking care of things?

We'll be fine. We're the only family she had. Walk to the end of the driveway, cross the road, and you'll see a path through the woods where you can pick up the river. It'll take you back to the field where your horse is.

Thanks.

Jonathan.

He stopped and looked back.

Take care of yourself, and be careful. And think about what Ella said, look for the truth, and when you find it, trust it, above all else.

Thank you, I will.

He walked through the wisps of drifting fog by the light of the moon. The long driveway stretching before him, the cool night air fresh on his face, and he felt lighter, the saddlebag on his back lighter, and he felt like he could walk forever. Like he'd want to. And he thought of Priscilla, cold and butchered on the table, her legs hanging over it, and he looked to the darkness.

He reached the end of the driveway and crossed the dirt road and found the pathway that dipped down through rock and scrub brush and back up again into an aged forest of hardwood and tall evergreens. He stopped. The forest silent. The fog heavier.

He had trouble seeing the pathway winding through the trees, and soon he began to see amongst the trees and the heavy fog, dark eyes watching him.

They're just wolves, he told himself, and he slid his shotgun around.

He continued along the path, the dark eyes fading in and out of the fog. And now he saw a young child, alone, dressed in thin and ragged clothes. First one, then several, some holding soundless newborn babies in their arms. He stopped, the fog taking the images. He walked again, down a hill to a small valley where he could hear the sounds of running water. He felt nauseous, and he tried to focus on the sounds of the water.

He stopped, there was a sound, and he wondered, what was that?

It was just a little man. Tiny. Standing in the hole of a tree. What? said the tiny man.

Nothing, said Jonathan. He wanted a cold drink of river water, badly, and he walked on.

And now the dark eyes reappearing. The children reappearing, silent and without emotion. Dead it seemed. Plague dead, and yet, watching him.

More reappeared, and more yet, the woods filling up with them. The displaced and unwanted. So many. He stopped and bent over, his shoulder leaning against a tree, and he vomited, his retching echoing in the cold quiet forest. He stood and ran the sleeve of his Mac across his mouth, and he began to walk again, trying to focus on the sound of the water. He stopped. Through the fog he saw an old man riding a horse, trailing another one behind him. He listened again for the sounds of the rippling water, and he began to walk toward it, and as he did, the river came into view. He focused harder, trying to keep to the path, trying to reach the river.

He bumped into the shoulder of a man leaning against a tree. Sorry, said Jonathan. Excuse me.

Of course, said the man. He was wearing a purple vest, a green sports jacket, red pants, and a brown trilby hat tilted on an angle. A cigarette, mostly smoked down, hung from his lips. He stepped aside and Jonathan walked past. Are you lost?

Jonathan stopped and looked back, but the man was gone.

The man took a drag of his cigarette and dropped his wrist over his crossed legs, the cigarette burning down between his fingers. Well?

Jonathan looked up at the man sitting on the overhanging limb of a large tree. No.

No?

No.

Perhaps you should go home?

Jonathan stared at the man. He looked over his shoulder in the direction of the running water. He looked back at the man.

Well?

I don't know.

No?

No.

Why? Is your fear not greater than your desire?

Jonathan looked again over his shoulder. He could hear the river. He needed a drink. He looked back, but the man was gone again.

Then tell me this, said the man, now standing behind Jonathan, leaning his mouth close to Jonathan's ear. Is there true worth in your desire? He ran his finger down Jonathan's chest. And does your heart have the capacity to hold it? Or, is it made of other clay?

Jonathan looked back, but the man wasn't there. Through the fog he saw again the old man riding the horse, trailing the other one, riding back the way he'd just come. The thin man was there, sitting sideways on the trailing horse, his legs crossed. He tipped his hat and shouted, good luck, Jonathan.

Jonathan walked to the river and fell to his knees and vomited. He lifted his head and looked around, and he dunked his head into the cold river water.

The sound of a rifle shot woke Jonathan. He sat up and looked around and saw the old man from the night before dismounting his horse, the other horse still tethered behind his. There was no sign of the other man. The old man dropped to his knees next to a fallen deer, and Jonathan approached him from behind.

The trick, the old man said without looking back, is to bring em down without killin em. He took his hunting knife from its sheave and made a small cut on the side of the deer's neck. He bent forward and placed his mouth over the cut and began to suck the deer's blood.

He pinched the cut closed with his thumb and forefinger, and he looked back at Jonathan. Would you like some?

Jonathan shook his head.

You sure? Best damn vitamins you'll ever get.

I'm all right, thanks.

Suit yourself, and the old man ran his knife across the deer's neck.

The deer was dressed out, the meat cut into thin strips that hung from green tree limbs standing upright around the fire.

You want some more of this? The old man held forward his quart of whiskey.

No, I'm good, thanks, and Jonathan took a sip of whiskey from his tin cup. You mind if I ask you a question?

No, not at all, ask away. In my ninety-eight years on this good earth, there's little I haven't heard yet.

You're ninety-eight?

Yup, ninety-nine next month.

That'll be some day when you turn a hundred.

If I make it.

What are you planning on doing?

Oh, I don't know. I haven't thought about it much, to be honest. I suppose, I'd want a nice hot bath, maybe a good steak, a glass or two of expensive whiskey, and a cigar, a good one. Oh, and a woman, of course. He laughed. A patient one.

Jonathan smiled.

And then I'd ride out into the hills where I was born, and I'd lie down in the tall grass and never get back up.

Oh?

The old man took another sip of whiskey. Yup, I wouldn't think, being a hundred, things could get much better after that.

Do you think it's wrong to kill yourself?

I didn't say I'd kill myself, I just thought it might be nice to go out with a smile on my face, that's all.

No, I didn't think you did. That was my question.

Oh, I see. Why? You're not thinking of it are ya?

No.

Good. I wouldn't think you would. You seem a little young yet for that. But I'll tell ya what, we all battle, at some point, or so it seems to me, a darkness and despair. A form of emptiness. Some survive, and some don't. And so I guess the question is, why? Is it because some are strong and others are weak? Maybe. But I have my doubts.

You do?

Yes, I do. He took another drink. He looked at Jonathan. When I was just a boy, we moved to a little nothing of a farm. It wasn't much at all. You'd ride up that long laneway, cross a creek and dog leg left to get to the house. And where that laneway bent, he used his right hand to illustrate a dog leg left, there was a slaughterhouse, on the outside of the turn, for horses. Pitiful. Flies everywhere. He held his hands up before him and indicated a space of about a foot and a half. Rats this big. It was terrible, all those horse carcasses piled up, one on top of the other, till you'd think the wagon was about to tip over. Headless, skinned, and butchered, their hooves still on.

Course as soon as we moved there my father wouldn't have anything to do with it, bein how he was into horses. He was a trainer, one of the very best. He didn't make out so good with horse tradin, but he was a great trainer. One time, he was havin trouble with a Hackney, a beautiful horse, but everyone said it was just too crazy in its head to be of any use to anyone. Not him. I guess he saw somethin in that horse others couldn't. I was just a small boy, but I can remember still, seein him with his fist up under that horse's head, holdin its tether tight as could be, runnin next to it, step for step, talkin to that horse the whole time, the horse's head up high, its wild eyes watchin my father. He did it for days. Over and over.

I never did know what was wrong with that horse, but it ended up being one of the best show horses around those parts. It was somethin to see. It truly was. His name was Meredith Jesse. Hell of a man, my father.

Well, of course, he tore that slaughterhouse down, cleared everythin away, like you'd never know it was ever there. New sod and everythin.

We had this big pasture at the front of the house, and my father, he'd tell me to go fetch such and such a horse, and I'd run down that long laneway and fetch the horse out of the pasture, and every single time, and I do mean every time, with any horse, over all the years I lived and worked there, I'd walk a horse up that beautiful laneway with the big willows hangin over it, the creek runnin under it, well, just as soon as I'd start around that dog leg, all hell would break loose. They'd spook, rearin up and shufflin back. Now why would that be? Why would a horse, years and years after he'd tore that slaughterhouse down, spook, in that very spot? Every time? Every horse?

I don't know, Jonathan said. But I have noticed horses can sense some things people can't.

That's right, they can. But what if some people were like that too? Able to sense those same types of things? Even just a little.

Like what?

Like that same kinda darkness.

How do you mean?

Well, imagine to a horse what that place must have seemed like. All darkness and death. And they knew it, too, that it was horses. Why else would they show such fear? In that very spot? Every time? And so I think perhaps some people can sense that as well, that same kinda overwhelming darkness and despair, beyond whatever you or I can see, or understand, and if that's true, then it no longer remains a question of strength, or weakness.

It doesn't?

Nope, it doesn't. The old man picked up his rifle and slid it into the scabbard and mounted the horse. He leaned forward and scratched behind the horse's right ear, and he looked down again at Jonathan. Even just a glimpse into the slaughterhouse of all man's time would be enough, wouldn't you think?

I guess it would.

Yes, it certainly would be. Horrible. Just horrible. But enough of this kinda talk, you're still a young man with your whole life in front of you, what could be better than that?

I don't know.

You don't know? Well, you had better know. This life requires of you to fight for and protect what's most meaningful to you, above all else, each and every day. And why should it not?

Jonathan stood. I'll do my best, thanks. And I hope you enjoy that day.

The old man smiled. And I hope you enjoy each and every one of yours. He kicked the horse and started on his way.

What about the other man?

The old man stopped the horse and looked back. Other man?

The thin one with the hat?

I'm travelling alone. When you get to be my age, you lose the habit of puttin up with other people's ways.

What about the deer?

Keep it. By the looks of that gun of yours, you won't be getting too many more. Be careful, Jonathan. The way of the road that you're on is the rule for all that travel upon it. And don't think there are any special cases, cause there's not. He turned the horse and rode on along the bank of the river.

Rachael crossed the backyard, a cup of coffee in her hand. I brought you coffee, Daddie.

He backed out from under the hood of their car. Thanks, sweetie. He took the coffee from her and took a sip. Feel like having a chat?

Sure.

On the swing?

Okay.

He took another sip and set the coffee on the edge of the car and they walked together to the swing set. Rachael took a seat on the closest one, and he gave her a push, the chain squeaking, and he thought, how do I do this?

He got her going higher, the squeak of the chain louder, and she thought, I hope everything's okay? Why's he want to chat? And even though she wished they would more, this was making her nervous. Everything okay, Daddie?

Yeah, sweetie. I just feel sad. I don't mean about Mom. Of course, I do about that, like you, but I mean, for you.

For me? She stopped pumping her legs.

Yes.

Why?

Because this isn't enough.

It's not?

No, you need more. And here he thought, he needed to tell her why, but he knew he wouldn't. How could he? A hundred times he'd wanted to, and he never could. It'd break him, he knew it would, even more than it would her. Regardless, he needed to make arrangements, and he said, I know you don't remember your aunt all that well.

Aunt Jean?

Yes, Aunt Jean. Your mother's sister.

We went there for a visit when I was little. She lives alone.

That's right. Well, I think we're going to go for another visit.

We are?

Yes.

Why?

I don't know, I just thought it might be nice to get away for a little bit. To get a break. We could both do with getting away. And you should get to know her better. I think your mother would like that.

How far is it?

Couple days.

Is that why you're fixing the car?

Yes.

When would we go?

I was thinking maybe Sunday.

Okay, I think a trip would be nice.

All right then, good. It's settled. He pushed her more, and he said, all the way to the moon.

And she said, yes, pumping her legs again, smiling, all the way to the moon and back.

Yes, he said, and back.

She was sitting on the metal step, smoking, looking at the house where she grew up. At the sad shape of it. She thought of everything that had happened. Her father would have shaken and beaten and banished his sorry raggedy ass down the road a long time ago. She needed to be smarter. And she would. And even though she couldn't beat his ass, she could shoot it. She could stab it, and she could set him on fire. And she would. She knew she would. So fuck you, Rooke. Your day is coming, and she flicked her smoke away, and she walked back into the trailer and closed the door.

He stood looking at the blood-stained grass, the image of Priscilla in his mind, her own knife sticking out from her, her legs now hanging dead weighted over the edge of a table.

He climbed the creek embankment and walked through the tall grass stopping when he saw Destiny, gutted in the night, the bones of her large chest cavity, bleach white, bright red blood stains, hundreds of flies swarming under the morning sun.

He looked toward the crossroads and the slight breeze moving through the branches of the trees that lined the road. He'd come too far. He knew he had. He looked in the direction of Urram Hill, and he thought of his mother. He thought again of the violations of Priscilla. He looked down at Destiny. Where does one thing stop and the other start? He didn't know. His anger real and not any less for not knowing.

PART FOUR

The sun was high in a dark blue sky, and Jonathan continued walking with his jacket folded through the strap of the saddlebag, the shotgun strapped over his back and tucked under his left arm.

On either side of the road began to appear large outcroppings of shield rock streaked with black and pink and where alder bushes, raspberry bushes, and trees grew from crevices.

He saw ancient trees grown too tall and heavy for their rocky moorings, having fallen onto their sides, great circular walls of exposed roots and dirt pointing to the sky.

He walked past dark and vacant lakes.

He walked past narrow, long stretches of washed-out lowlands, where sun-bleached trees still stood, dead and broken.

He walked a long straight stretch of road and came to a hard bend to the right. He walked the turn, and he came to a crossroad. He looked up the road running north. He looked south. There was nothing. Just more emptiness and quiet, the sun hard on the gravel, and he stayed on the road he was on.

Where you goin, son?

Jonathan looked back. It was an older woman with a cigarette. Short cropped white hair. High black rubber boots. A dress and a heavy sweater. I'm looking for a pickup. A red one.

Well, you're about to enter the Valley of Dry Bones, where anything is possible. So, you just might find it, here in this place where roads travel in all directions, from this to that, and that to this, and where death itself leaks from the dark cold earth.

Have you seen it?

I've seen it rising to the very loin.

I meant my pickup.

There's a steep hill ahead, that levels off and runs between tall pines and large rocks, before dropping off again to the other side of nowhere.

My truck's there?

Your truck isn't the question. You'll have it by then.

I will?

Yes. But that is still not the question, is it? The question is, is that where you'll wanna be?

Jonathan didn't answer, and they stood looking at one another.

The old woman took a last drag from her smoke and pitched it to the road. Son, I have yet to see the glory without the darkness. She looked down the road in the direction of The Valley of Dry Bones. It's a double hook, she whispered, that's just what it is. She looked back at Jonathan. On your way, son, for what do I know? I am but a woman, sharpened to the very edge of stone. Much like your mother, I suppose. And keep in mind, too, there is never just one wasp in any wasp's nest. Good luck to you.

He came to a short hill, the road bending back left again. After a while, he came to another hill that took him down to a valley, the road seen climbing again in the distance. He stopped. His father's pickup was in a ditch before a large gravel pull-off area next to a natural spring pouring out from the crevice of an outcropping of granite rock. To the left of the spring toward the back of the pull-off area was a nineteen thirties covered truck. Painted on the side of the faded tan tarp were the words, Wakefield's Traveling Freak Show.

He tried the driver-side door of his father's pickup and it opened. The keys were there. There was nothing on the front seat, and he looked in the back. On the floor was his father's .303 and a box of ammunition. He swung the saddlebag off his shoulder and tossed it onto the front seat. He unhooked the shotgun and placed it next to the saddlebag. He got in and tried the truck and it started.

A tall man with a beard and thick slicked back fair hair, walked toward Jonathan. Looks like you could use a hand?

Yes, I could. Thank you.

I'm Wakefield. He pointed back toward the truck. Like the truck says.

I'm Jonathan. I'll push if you don't mind jumping in?

My thoughts exactly.

Wakefield got in the cab and watched Jonathan position himself at the front of the truck. Jonathan nodded and

Wakefield dropped it in reverse, the tires spinning, shooting gravel out behind the truck. Jonathan tried rocking the truck back and forth and it still wouldn't come, the front tires too far down into the ditch, the bottom of the truck grounding out on the road.

Wakefield turned the engine off and stepped out. I gotta chain in the truck. That'll do it. How'd you get it stuck?

I didn't.

Oh?

I found it like that. I been looking for it.

It was stolen?

Yup.

It wasn't there when I pulled up to sleep, so it hasn't been there that long. We'll get that chain on her. I'll just let the freaks know first, otherwise, they'll be tumblin and cryin all over one another wondering where I am.

Freaks?

Hmm, like in the carnival, you know. We're on our way to one now. Course, business hasn't been so good lately, and I been thinkin of letting em go. Maybe get myself setup in some other line of work. Times aren't what they once were and freaks don't seem to draw like they used to.

Where?

Where what?

Where would you let them go?

Oh, I dunno. Out there somewhere, I suppose. To tell ya the truth, it don't really matter that much, freaks seem to find their own way better than most, least ways that's been my experience. They seem naturally inclined to find that one person, or group of people, with an affinity for the wounded and disfranchised. Personally, I couldn't get any more disinterested in what happens to em.

Wakefield walked toward his truck and a nineteen fifties GM Silversides bus pulled up and stopped. Painted on the fluted aluminum cladding were the words, Red Light Express.

Jonathan walked up and stood next to Wakefield and together they watched a series of girls exit the bus, all different shapes and sizes, some tall and some short, some young and some older, fat ones and thin ones. The last one out was a large woman with a long colorful dress and white sandals. She had large pink curlers in her hair and was holding a drink in a large light green plastic cup. She looked and shooed the girls away gathering around Jonathan and Wakefield. Go on, girls, hurry up and find a bush, we need to get back on the road as soon as possible. She looked at Jonathan and Wakefield. Pleased to meet you, I'm Addie, and these are my girls.

I'm Wakefield.

Addie shook his hand. Nice to meet you, Wakefield. This your son?

Nope. We just met. That's his truck there stuck in the ditch.

Addie shook Jonathan's hand. You're a handsome one. What's your name, son?

Jonathan.

Are they all whores? asked Wakefield.

Of course, they're all whores, what'd ya think they were?

I figured they were.

The plumbing is out on the bus and every one of those girls is ready to explode.

What'ya doin out this way? Wakefield asked.

There's a mine openin up, and we're on our way there now.

That's what you do? Jonathan asked. Move from one place to the next?

Yup, just like that, one place to the next.

Several of the girls gathered around the back of Wakefield's truck, one of them pulling back the tarp flap, looking inside, where she saw the World's Tallest Man, the World's Shortest Man, the World's Fattest Man, the Half-Man Half-Woman Person, Fish Boy, Lion Man, and Elephant Girl, sitting on benches before a single burning candle playing cards.

Wakefield slapped the tarp shut. That'll cost ya each a buck.

The girls laughed and walked away, all but the one Wakefield was speaking to, who leaned closer and grabbed his crotch. There you go, Daddie, paid in full.

Addie stood at the open bus door. C'mon girls, if you've done your business, back on the bus. Let's go.

On their way to the bus, several girls stopped and gathered around Jonathan. One of the girls, wearing a light blue satin dress and white high heels, leaned into Jonathan and ran her hand through his hair. You ever have a girl other than your own mother tell you how handsome you are?

You're strong, too, aren't ya? said another one of the whores running her hand down his arm.

Jonathan looked at Addie, talking with several of the girls by the open bus door.

A third girl, wearing a low white blouse, pressed herself to Jonathan. Would you like to see em?

The girl in the dress smiled and pulled the other girl's top out, away from her. Milky white and pink, aren't they?

Another girl, with long blond hair, ran her hand down Jonathan's back. I bet you could ride me till the bell rung, huh?

The girl in the light blue dress linked her arm through the arm of the girl wearing the white blouse, her other arm linked through Jonathan's. Why don't we all go on the bus together? We got time yet.

They walked toward the bus and as they did they heard the sound of heavy tires on the gravel road. They stopped and looked.

Addie and the other girls stepped back past the bus and looked.

Men in military fatigues jumped from two nineteen eighties army trucks with the tarps rolled back.

Addie leaned into the bus. Skiver, she said to the driver, I think we're gonna be here for a while yet.

The men were off the truck, mingling with the girls, opening bottles of whiskey and cans of beer, some already paired off with girls and walking onto the bus.

What's the occasion?

Jonathan looked at a nun standing next to him holding a rope with a Jersey cow tied to the other end.

I don't know, other than my truck getting stuck, I can't think of one.

You need a hand? The cow bawled and stepped back. The nun tugged the rope. Never mind, Jezebel, you're just fine. She shouted at a group of men. Hey, you, you, and you. Give us a hand. I guarantee you those girls will wait.

One of the military men looked at another man standing next to him. He slapped the man's arm. C'mon, Sanchez, let's give em a hand.

The men she indicated, and several others, followed the nun and Jonathan toward the pickup. Jonathan got in and started the truck. The men squeezed in tight together at the front of the truck.

Jonathan dropped it into reverse.

One of the men counted it down, one ... two ... three, and they lifted and pushed the front of the truck, and Jonathan gunned the engine, and the truck ran out of the ditch and onto the road.

He pulled the truck up to the side of the road and turned it off. He got out and stood next to the nun. Thank you. I would have never thought they'd have done that.

Oh, of course, they would, the world is filled with good people just in need of a little push to do the right thing.

I guess.

The crowd at the side of the road fell silent. Nobody moved. Everyone stood watching as a long line of rough riders on horseback approached up the road. The ghosts of men. They watched them draw closer. Each man a perfect embodiment of some form of death with torn and bloodstained clothes, matted and braided hair, tattooed bodies and tattooed faces, faces painted with the blood of others, guns tucked into their belts, scabbard rifles, sabers, and bowie knifes, the horses, too, caked in dried blood and earth, some painted, shrunken dried skulls hanging from thin ropes tied around their necks, their bulging dark eyes fierce in their large heads, straining with strength and terror, their nostrils flaring, scenting the foreign smells of these silent strangers, this insult of sanctity, a lack of desperation and death among them. Like some strange collective falsehood. A mistrusting.

The riders turned off the road and rode up a wide trail that cut through the woods, disappearing just as silently as they appeared.

A whore looked at the nun. Did you see that? It looked like something right out of the past, did it not? Or maybe it was a dream? It was kinda spooky, though, wasn't it?

Yes, it was. But you're right about the past being little more than a dream, for it is created new each day.

It is?

Oh, of course, it is. How could it not be? Retribution and renewal. It can happen to each of us, each and every day.

It can?

The nun put her hand to the side of the whore's face. Faith, my dear, and she ran her hand down the whore's face.

In God?

Yes, in God, and with God's love. See the garden, it's there. And just because you can't find your way there, does not mean it is not there. I'm Sister Francis. A keeper of the garden. Your garden.

Nice to meet you, Sister. I'm Angel.

Angel?

Yes, Angel Proper.

Wakefield exited the bus and walked toward them. Where are you goin with a cow, for God's sake?

The nun looked at Wakefield. Not for God's sake, but in God's name. I picked up sweet Jezebel here from some friends of the convent. She was a gift.

He looked at Jonathan. I see you got your truck clear of the ditch.

With the help of Sister—.

Francis.

She pushed it out? Or the cow did? Wakefield laughed.

Neither, said the nun, I simply enlisted a few of those kind, but otherwise, engaged gentlemen.

Are you going far? Jonathan asked the nun.

It's a way yet, yes.

Can I give you a ride?

I have Jezebel?

That's all right.

How are ya gonna get a cow up there? asked Wakefield.

C'mon, I'll show ya.

Together Jonathan and Wakefield walked toward Wakefield's truck. And better yet, said Wakefield, why the hell would you want to?

Fish Boy and Elephant Girl had their heads sticking out from the back of the truck watching the party at the side of the road. They saw Wakefield approaching and they tucked their heads back inside. He slapped the tarp closed. What the hell are ya doin? We ain't givin away no free shows. Keep your damn freaky-selves in there.

The sides of the truck had three rows of two-by-eights and together Jonathan and Wakefield removed the bottom one from each side. They returned to the pickup and Jonathan opened the tailgate. They placed the boards against it and let the other ends drop to the ground.

Jonathan looked at the nun. Does she follow you?

She has so far.

All right, give it a try.

The nun walked up the planks and gave the rope a tug. The cow didn't move. The nun tugged again, and it still wouldn't move.

Move to the side. I'll be right back.

Jonathan walked to the trees and broke off a young white birch branch and walked back again. Ready? Give her a good tug.

The nun pulled the rope and Jonathan brought the branch down on the backside of the cow. It moved forward, and when it stopped midpoint, Jonathan brought the branch down again, and the cow stepped onto the truck.

Wakefield and Jonathan removed the boards, and Jonathan closed the tailgate. They walked back to Wakefield's truck and returned the boards.

Well, I guess that's it. You're on your way then, said Wakefield.

Jonathan shook Wakefield's hand. It was nice to meet you. Good luck with the shows.

Thanks. Now that you found your truck, ya headin home?

Nope.

Oh?

There's a few things I have to do yet.

All right, well, whatever it is, good luck to ya.

Thanks, and Jonathan walked to the pickup and opened the driver's door. He looked at Sister Francis. Coming?

Sister Francis looked at Angel. What about you?

Me?

Yes, you. You seem ready to start a new and better day.

Angel looked at Addie joining Wakefield by his truck. Oh, I don't know.

Come on, Angel, come and start fresh. You'll be well taken care of, I can promise you that.

Angel looked again at Addie, talking to Wakefield, hooking her arm through his and walking toward the bus.

Sister Francis opened the door and Angel started to walk toward it.

Addie looked and yelled, Angel.

Angel got in and Sister Francis closed the door and stood in front of it.

What'ya think you're doing? Get outta that truck.

One of the girls and a soldier walked up to Addie, and the whore asked, is there still room in the bus?

Try the last one on the right, Parker's been in there since we got here. She's probably sleepin, the lazy slut.

Addie looked back toward the pickup. Angel, get your unappreciative bony little ass out of that truck, right this minute. She walked forward and stood before Sister Francis.

She'll do no such thing, said Sister Francis.

Addie looked past her. Angel, get out. Right this minute.

The soldiers and other whores began to turn and look.

Wakefield walked up and stood next to Addie.

Angel? She looked back at the others. Someone get her outta there, right this goddamn minute.

No one moved.

Wakefield placed his hand on Addie's arm, and she shrugged it away. Angel Proper, if you know what's good for you, you'll get outta that truck.

There were tears in Angel's eyes, and she looked away.

I believe the girl is staying right where she is, said Sister Francis, and I would suggest you let it go.

She's right, Addie, said Wakefield. Let it go.

No. She leaned toward Wakefield. She's one of my best money-makers.

A few of the soldiers began to walk toward the truck.

Sister Francis looked at the men, opened the door, and got in. The men stopped, standing next to Addie and Wakefield.

Addie stepped forward and leaned into the open window. Fine, ya little bitch, go. Who needs ya, anyway?

Sister Francis looked at Jonathan, and Jonathan dropped the truck into gear, Addie stepping back. You just remember this, Angel, you're a whore, and you always will be. Do you hear me? The truck pulled away, and Addie followed it. And no amount of misguided, misdirected, God-fearing nun-cunts can change that. Ya unappreciative little slut.

Wakefield joined Addie and together they watched the truck climb the long steep hill.

Rachael had a ball, and she was throwing it against the side of the garage and catching it. She looked toward the house. He won't tell it, Alice, but I know he's sick. I've seen his pills. She threw the ball again and caught it. I don't want to go live with that old woman, I think she stinks. I remember her. And she's a little mean, and she doesn't read books. She caught the ball again and looked back to the house. *Thus, grew the tale of Wonderland,* she said. She threw the ball and caught it again. *Thus slowly, one by one, Its quaint events were hammered out.* She threw the ball more. *And now the tale is done, And home we steer, a merry crew, Beneath the setting sun.* She caught the ball and threw it, over and over, until the sun was low and setting, and it was time to make supper.

The second 'l' in the blue neon sign, Lamplight, flicked on and off above the entrance to the bar.

The pickup stopped.

They might have something to eat, said Jonathan.

I'm fine, said Sister Francis. What about you, Angel?

I could eat something, but I don't got any money. Addie kept it for me.

That's all right, said Jonathan. I'll get it, and he turned into the gravel lot and parked beneath an overhanging oak tree on the right side of the lot. What would you like?

Whatever you're having is fine with me.

I won't be long. He got out and reached into the back and picked up his shotgun and put the strap over his head. He walked past a scattering of old cars and pickups. He looked to his right and saw Holly standing smoking on the metal stair of her trailer parked next to the bar.

A tall thin man walked out of the bar.

Holly flicked her cigarette away and walked into the trailer.

The tall thin man walked to the trailer and climbed the metal stair. He entered the trailer and closed the door.

At the entrance to the bar was a young boy with a brush cut and a heavily freckled face holding a cardboard box with a sign taped to the side that read, chiks 4 Saal 50¢.

I'll buy one.

Fifty cent.

I can't take it with me, if that's all right?

What'ya want it for then?

You can keep it for me.

I can't keep it for ya, I'm tryin to sell em.

127

Jonathan handed the boy fifty cents. Sell it again if you want to.

Thanks, mister.

The room was filled with mostly men, some sitting at the bar, some standing, and others sitting at high round tables. The ceiling was low, and the room heavy with smoke. The bartender, a large man with long red hair and a long beard, wearing a white dirty apron, placed a mug of draft beer in front of Leonard and picked up Leonard's dirty plate and cutlery. Anything else?

Leonard turned and looked at the door opening. He smiled.

Well?

He looked at the bartender. No, that's it, thanks.

In the open back room, Rooke and several other men stood at a bar, the card playing table empty of players.

Jonathan walked to the main bar and waited for the bartender. He looked over the room, at the few farmers and day laborers, the rough and ready, the few women there, one large woman sitting at a high round table with purple stretch pants pulled tight and spilling over her stool. She laughed and drank her beer, talking with two other women and two men, both men with long hair, their jeans and white t-shirts stained with grease.

Leonard walked past Jonathan and out the door.

He stopped and looked at the young boy. What'ya got there?

Fifty cent.

Leonard dug into his pocket and took out a dollar and handed it to the boy.

I don't got change. But you can have two.

Leonard looked into the box. See that one?

The boy lowered the box and looked at the chick Leonard was pointing to. That's the runt. You want that one?

Leonard picked it up.

Is that the one you want? The runt?

Ya know what ya gotta do with em?

The boy shook his head.

Cull em.

Cull em?

That's it, cull em, and Leonard pressed his thumb down, crushing the chick's skull.

The boy said, you ain't gettin your money back.

Can ya remember that?

Cull em, said the boy. Why do I gotta do that?

It makes the whole stronger.

At the far end of the wall was a man sitting on the ground leaning against the wall, his arms hooked around his knees, his head down. He turned and looked at Leonard walking through the parking lot.

Leonard spotted Jonathan's truck and stopped. My my, he said, and he walked toward it, the small trailer behind him swaying back and forth to the rhythm of the tall thin man fucking Holly.

Is that it? the bartender asked.

And a coffee.

The bartender left, and the man standing next to Jonathan turned and looked at him. He had a glass eye that angled toward the ceiling. My name's Bob.

Bob?

Bob Caygeon, pleased to meet ya.

Nice to meet you, Mr. Caygeon.

Ya gettin it to go?

Yes, sir, I am.

Well, be careful out there.

Oh?

These are strange times, with stranger ones comin yet.

People keep telling me that.

Because they know it. They can sense it, even if they can't see it, or know the reason why.

What's that?

This restricting. A contracting. It's here now and it's happening. The deserving and undeserving. Both. And there's only one thing that can stop it.

What's that?

Just one, and nothin else, and the man placed his hand on Jonathan's chest. An expansion. Only that.

Leonard placed his hands on the roof of the pickup and leaned into the open driver's side window. Evening, ladies.

Angel and Sister Francis turned and looked.

It's a nice night, is it not?

Can we help you?

Well, I don't know. You've got two choices, I suppose. You can get out, or you can come with me. Part way, at least.

Excuse me?

Leonard held up two fingers of his left hand. He wiggled his fingers. Two.

This is not your truck, said Sister Francis.

No, it's not, but it is the truck I'm taking. He pushed back from the truck and opened the door and got in and shut the door.

Angel shifted away from Leonard.

What do you think you're doing? said Sister Francis.

I told ya—and what the hell is that damn cow doin in the truck?

Sister Francis leaned past Angel and tried to remove the keys. Leonard grabbed her wrist.

She looked at his washed blue eyes, and she saw nothing there but the cold hard edge of not caring. Total indifference. I would appreciate it, she said, if you'd let go, and she tried to pull her arm away. You're hurting me. She leaned forward and smashed her other hand down onto his chest.

Leonard opened the door and dragged the nun over the top of Angel and out the door.

The nun screamed and kicked, and he placed his hand over her mouth and forced her to the ground. He placed his knee on her chest. He reached into his pocket and took out his knife. He opened it and put it to her throat. He looked around. The young boy was no longer at the front of the bar. The trailer had stopped rocking. He looked back at the nun, her frightened eyes searching his eyes for any sign of hope that might appear. There was none.

I guess you'd like to know God? Is that it? He heard the passenger door open, and he bent over the nun, lowering his head to the ground, watching Angel through the space beneath the truck and the ground running toward the road. He looked back at Sister Francis, and he wondered how it was his body could feel her conviction, her spiritual current, because he could, the very same as if she were to hold it out in her hands before him, saying, here, this is it, it's warm, isn't it? Take it. He smiled and tilted his head, and he opened up her neck.

He ran fast through the dark woods, effortless, and without error.

On the road, Angel was running. She looked back. There was only darkness. She turned back around, and he was there, on the road before her, waiting. She screamed. He reached out and pulled her to him. She screamed again and he covered her mouth and he pulled her head back. You're a whore, aren't ya?

She tried to bite his hand.

Well, of course you are, and you shouldn't have been in that truck, should ya? Trying not to be a whore like that. He moved his mouth closer to the side of her face. Not only that, you're a coward. Leaving that poor old nun when all she tried to do was to help ya. You should be ashamed of yourself. You really should. And he ran his knife across her neck and let her body fall to the road.

Whore blood, he thought, running dark in the dark night.

He walked back to the truck and got in. He closed the door and put it in reverse, the cow slamming hard against the cab. He put the truck in drive and pulled up to the road. He stopped and looked left, at Angel dead on the road, and he turned right.

He stopped the truck and stepped out and walked to the back of it and opened the tailgate. He got back in and looked in the rear-view mirror, the heavy blue exhaust smoke pumping in the night air. He hit the gas, and the truck sped forward, the cow launching from the back—a cow flying. And such a sight as that, as if suspended in the night, before hitting the road, its back legs buckling and breaking, tumbling and rolling, like some irregular black and white shaped thing doe-ray-me-ing down the dark, vacant road.

A man in a white shirt and black pants with a wide black leather belt pulled tight walked up to Rooke and bent down.

She's what?

Yup.

Shit. That little bitch, and he got up and hurried to the door.

Jonathan held his coffee and two steak sandwiches wrapped in white paper napkins in his hands. He leaned his back against the door and pushed it open and walked outside.

The door opened again and Rooke stopped and stood next to Jonathan. He looked at the trailer. The door was open. Fuck, he said, and he looked at Jonathan. Where the hell did she go?

Jonathan looked at Rooke. Who?

Rooke paused, studying Jonathan. Never fuckin mind.

Jonathan watched Rooke walk to the trailer and look inside. He looked back at Jonathan. Ya must of seen her?

Nope, I didn't. I just got out here before you did, and I didn't see anyone.

Jonathan walked toward his pickup. He stopped and looked at Sister Francis still bleeding from her opened neck. He knelt down, and he looked up, and saw the boy with the box of chicks standing at the edge of the woods. Did you see who did this?

The boy shook his head.

Jonathan approached the boy. Are you sure? It's all right, you can tell me if you did.

I ain't seen nobody, said the boy. I was goin home and I saw her like that.

Here, and Jonathan handed the boy the two steak sandwiches.

You ain't hungry?

Not anymore, I'm not.

Jonathan walked to the road and stopped, there were several wild dogs standing over Angel's body. They looked up and furled their upper lips and growled. Jonathan walked forward, the dogs lowering their heads, growling louder, showing their teeth. He stopped and unshouldered the shotgun and leveled it at the dogs. Behind him came the sick bawl of the cow. He turned and looked, and as he did, one of the dogs rushed forward and jumped, Jonathan turning and firing, the dog spinning in the air and landing on the road. At the sound of the gun, the other dogs backed away, their heads lowered.

Jonathan turned and walked toward the cow keeping an eye out behind him.

Rooke's Impala sped out of the parking lot and passed Jonathan, swerving around the mangled cow. Jonathan watched the Impala drive away. He looked toward the woods and the eyes he saw there. You can wait, and he took out his knife and pushed it deep into the center of the cow's neck, twisting the knife until the cow's throat was opened.

He walked back toward Angel. There were more dogs, all fighting for the right to drive their diseased and blackened teeth into her flesh, and when they did, shaking their heads so violently they spun her like some straw doll, one way, and back the other, down the gravel road.

Jonathan fired as he walked, two dogs going down, one of them able to drag itself into the ditch. The other dogs fleeing to the woods.

A group of men gathered at the open bar door, highlighted in neon, watching Jonathan pick up Angel and walk with her over his shoulder.

Ya think he just gunned her down?

Looks like it.

Ya ever seen that one before?

Nope.

Me neither.

I don't think he did it.

Why's that?

Maybe Rooke done her.

Rooke?

Her throat's been cut. You can see it trailing out of her from here.

I can see it too.

Maybe he done that first and then he shot her?

Why would he cut her throat and then shoot her?

Probably the dogs.

That killed her?

Nope. That he fired on.

You could hear em.

What? The dogs?

Yup.

Somebody done her.

Ya know, she's gone again, don't ya?

Who?

Holly?

Yup.

That was her?

Nope, but she's gone all the same. So is Rooke.

If it wasn't Rooke, who done it?

I bet he does her this time.

I bet he does too.

He'd better not.

Dumb bastard, can't even keep her locked up right.

We're fucked now.

Nope, that's the point, ain't it? Not anymore we're not. Not if he does her.

Fuckin Rooke.

Damn right, fuckin Rooke.

Jonathan walked in the night and stopped. The shield rock forming and rising on both sides of the road. He set Angel down on the rocks to his right. He climbed the tiered rock and stopped at a wide gap. He looked at the dark outline of the trees across the road. Dark clouds drifting. An owl calling.

He pulled Angel up over the rocks and rolled her into the gap, and he covered her with small rocks.

He wiped the sweat from his face and looked down the road in the direction of what? He didn't know.

His mother?

Probably not—not this far.

He looked in the direction of Urram Hill, and he wanted answers.

Answers written in blood.

They always are, and he walked on.

PART FIVE

Faint sounds of fiddle music drifting in the dark. In the trees. Jonathan stopping and listening, the long carrying notes of a fiddle being played well, holding him there.

He walked more, and he came upon the fiddler in the night, a young man wearing a baggy black suit, a white shirt, a brown wool cap, and standing in the middle of the dark road.

There was an old man with him, at the side of the road, wearing dark wayfarer sunglasses, his hands clasped behind his back, his feet turned out, his knees bent forward, dancing a slow shuffle two-step. The man smiling, a silver tooth shinning.

The fiddler ended his tune. I'm Charlie.

The men stood listening, the last notes of the song resounding in the dark, under the moonlight, and drifting gone, leaving them in silence.

And right here, this is the one and only Mr. McCabe.

The old man nodded.

Jonathan asked, did you see a pickup come by?

A pickup?

A red '62 Ford.

Well, I don't think one did, no. Did it, Mr. McCabe?

No. Not one.

What about a car? A black Impala?

Well, yeah, there was one of those, said the fiddler.

They was goin slow, like they were looking for somethin, said Mr. McCabe.

It was a girl, said Jonathan.

A girl? said the fiddler.

Who they were looking for.

Yup, it was one of those, for sure, they was lookin for, said Mr. McCabe.

He mentioned that? said the fiddler.

Did, said Mr. McCabe.

Thanks, said Jonathan.

No trouble at all, said the fiddler.

Can I ask you something?

Of course, you can, said the fiddler.

Do you always play your fiddle out here in the middle of the night?

It's a livin.

A living?

Unhuh. We accept donations, contributions, anything really.

Do you get many people coming by here at night like this?

You'd be surprised.

I guess I would.

Can I ask you somethin? said the fiddler.

Sure.

Did you like what you heard?

Yeah, I thought it was good. Really good, actually.

Thank you, said the fiddler. He smiled and nodded toward the upside-down cap on the road in front of Mr. McCabe.

Jonathan reached into his pocket and pulled out his money. He took a dollar from it and dropped it in the hat.

Thank you, but please, don't be modest.

Modest?

I thought you said you liked it?

I did.

Well, that's kinda insultin, don't ya think?

Insulting?

Right.

I can't afford anything more than that.

The young man reached under his coat and pulled out a long-barreled handgun. He cocked the hammer and pointed it at Jonathan. Well, I think you can, that is, if ya just reach down a little deeper into your heart, and you expand that, because, well, really, what else is there?

Are you robbing me?

You could look at it that way, I suppose, if you wanted to. We prefer to think of it as a forced appreciation tax.

Jonathan dropped his roll of bills into the hat.

No no no, now, that's just not necessary.

Mr. McCabe reached down and took out half of Jonathan's bills and held them back out to him.

It wouldn't be right to leave you out here broke and all alone like that, said the fiddler.

Jonathan took the money.

Is there anything else you'd like to hear?

Play whatever you like.

Here, now, don't go away mad, it's only money. Surely there must be somethin you'd like to hear?

Do you know Keane's Romance?

Aye, a lovely tune. It'd be a pleasure.

The fiddler holstered his gun and raised the fiddle to his chin. He began to play and Jonathan looked at the old man, his hands again behind his back, his feet moving at angles pointed out, his knees bent, and smiling his big toothy smile that stretched across his unshaven and heavily- lined face. And the fiddler played on in the night. For all the sadness, hidden in the dark. In the shadows. Waiting. And always there, or so it seemed. Jonathan walking. Remembering. The bones of a bird. The music drifting. Keep an eye on her. The darkness taking him. The music playing on.

Rachael was sleeping, in her chair, by the fire. Was she dreaming?

Probably she was.

And Alice came. In the room with her.

There now.

Rachael. Wake up and be here with me.

But no mother.

No other friends.

And soon your father too. In this dreaming.

Rachael.

And sometimes, this is all we have.

Is that not right, Alice?

Alice?

Wake up, Rachael.

This intersecting of hopes and dreams and aloneness. Alice called again, Rachael. Wee Rachael. Rachael the Reminder.

And how sad Rachael would be, knowing she missed her.

Alice.

Alice here.

Alice there and with her now.

Jonathan stopped. Past the trees to the left of a grassy laneway that cut south off the road was a small fire burning. The moonlight, highlighting the top of the trees.

He walked again looking beyond the trees trying to see who might be there. He walked past the spot where the fire was, and he cut into the woods.

He picked his way carefully through the woods stepping over dead fallen branches and making sure not to brush up against any low hanging ones. He came to the clearing, and he squatted down. He saw Holly sitting against a tree, tied and gagged. Rooke stretched out next to the fire sleeping. The ground was mostly pine needles, and he walked slowly, stepping carefully, until he was close to the fire and Rooke. He removed his knife and walked forward more. He saw his father's gun was sticking out of Rooke's belt. He put his knife away and took another step forward and squatted down next to Rooke. He reached slowly for his father's gun, and he slid it from Rooke's belt, pointing it at him.

What the fuck?

Jonathan stood checking the chamber of the gun. It was loaded. He pointed the gun back at Rooke.

Have you lost your fuckin mind? What the hell do you think you're doin?

Where'd you get this gun?

Fuck you.

Holly began to struggle, moaning and indicating something by nodding forward.

Jonathan backed up, keeping an eye on Rooke. Move and I'll shoot you. And don't think I won't. He pulled the rag down covering Holly's mouth.

He's got a gun in his boot.

Jonathan looked back at Rooke. Take it out and drop it on the ground.

Rooke leaned forward and pulled his pant leg over his boot and pulled the gun out.

Drop it to the ground.

Rooke didn't move.

Jonathan pulled the hammer back. Do it.

Rooke dropped the gun. What'ya want?

Kick the gun out.

He kicked at the gun. Well?

Untie me, Holly said to Jonathan.

He looked at Holly, at her heavily damaged face, her swollen lips and eyes, a deep cut running above her right eye to the bridge of her nose.

Do it, Holly told him.

Jonathan took his knife out and cut Holly's ropes, and she took off running toward Rooke.

Stop.

She kept running.

Keep away from that gun.

She stopped and looked back at Jonathan, walking toward her, the gun pointed at her.

She turned and ran again.

Don't.

She picked up the gun.

Put it down.

That's my girl, don't let that boy come in here and threaten us. Shoot em.

Jonathan said to her again, put the gun down.

She looked at Jonathan.

Do it, said Rooke. Shoot the little prick.

Jonathan held his hand out. Give it to me.

Holly turned and looked at Rooke. You sick fucking bastard asshole, and she lifted the gun and fired, emptying the rounds into him. She dropped her arm to her side.

Jonathan stepped forward and took the gun from her hand. Have you ever been to New Acadia?

Holly looked at Jonathan. What?

He held up the Colt. Where'd he get this?

He traded for it.

For what?

What do you think?

When?

At the bar.

With who?

Holly looked at Rooke.

With who?

Some kid.

A kid?

Yeah, about our age. Maybe a little older.

Do you know where he went?

No, why would I know that? She walked up to Rooke and bent down and reached into his pocket looking for the car keys. She found them and stood. She looked at Jonathan. Thanks.

For what?

You didn't have to untie me, but you did.

Are you okay? Your face doesn't look so good.

Thanks.

No, I didn't mean—.

I know what you meant. What's your name?

Jonathan.

I'm Holly.

Jonathan looked at Rooke, at the blood running from him, pooling on the pine needles. Who was he?

An asshole. That's who. What were you doing out here?

Looking for the person that had this gun.

Why? They steal it?

And my dad's truck.

Where's the truck now?

I don't know.

Can you drive?

Of course, I can drive.

Good, and she tossed the keys at Jonathan and walked to the fire and picked up the end of a burning branch sticking out from the fire. She walked back to Rooke and dropped the branch on him. Burn in hell, you sick fuckin prick.

She looked at Jonathan. Let's go.

They walked to the Impala and got in. Jonathan looked back at Rooke, burning under a tree. He put the car in drive and pulled up to the road. The light in the trees, still there and brighter yet. Jonathan looked at Holly. Which way?

I dunno, you tell me. You're lookin for your dad's truck, right?

Right.

So, which way?

No idea.

Left. When things don't go right, go left.

Jonathan smiled. Is that right?

Go left, and don't be an asshole. There's enough of those in the world already.

I'll do my best, and he turned left, the darkness of the night taking the Impala.

They drove on, the car low and heavy, the headlights highlighting the thick rows of trees on either side of the road, and he looked at Holly leaning against the door sleeping, the light of the moon reaching to her, her beaten face, her long hair. And he wondered, how could anyone do such a thing? He looked back at the road, at the headlights on the gravel.

Hey.

Jonathan looked.

How old are you?

Sixteen. You?

Seventeen. She turned away and looked out her window, at the cold air of the night, the moonlight in the moving branches of the trees, and she heard a whisper there, you can't have everything. You can't fix everything. But you can try, she whispered back, and with tears in her eyes, she slept again, the moon and the stars and all the world, falling away, the car there, moving on, rumbling and heavy in the dark night.

He woke on the couch and sat up. He listened to Rachael making breakfast in the kitchen. He looked at her empty chair. Today, he thought. He rubbed his hands over his face and through his hair. Do it today.

Jonathan woke, the sun in his eyes, and he dropped the visor. Holly wasn't there. He looked out his side window at a long row of tall evergreens.

He walked past the trees and came to a rocky cliff. She was there below him, standing with her back to him in a wide river feeding into a large lake. He moved to the edge of the cliff and leaned against a tree and looked at Holly's long hair moving gently in the current. He watched her gather it in her arm, and he squinted to see better the crisscrossing of red welts and scars that covered her back. The fresh ones wet and glistening in the sun, overlaid upon the patchwork of older, faded ones. She leaned forward and dunked her head under the water and tried to scrub it clean with her hands. She flipped her head back, her hair landing on the water behind her.

She turned and she saw Jonathan. How long have you been there?

Not long.

Really?

Yup.

The way down is over there.

He looked to where she pointed.

She backed into the river until the water was just below her shoulders. She watched him walk to the edge of the cliff and start down the pathway. C'mon, cowboy, hurry up.

Cowboy?

You walk like one. The water's warm.

He sat on a large rock next to Holly's clothes hanging from a bush, and he undid one boot and slipped it off and then the other one. He took his socks off and stood and pulled his t-shirt over his head. He looked at Holly.

Go on, I won't look.

Turn around.

She turned around, and he undid his belt and pulled his pants and boxers off. He stepped into the water. He stepped back. I thought you said it was warm?

She laughed. It's not that bad. Get in here. She heard a splash, and she turned around and waited for him to surface.

149

He broke from the water just before her. It's cold, he said, and he cleared the water from his face.

She looked at the pale smooth skin of his chest, his raised collarbones stretching across his wide shoulders, her hands moving back and forth slowly over the surface of the dark silky river water. She looked again at his face. He looked older than what he was. His dark eyes.

Are you standing on a rock?

She shook her head, her hands still moving over the surface of the water.

You're taller than I thought.

Tall enough, I guess. She turned and looked at the lake. Let's swim out there.

Jonathan remained looking at the water gently washing over the tops of her breasts, the full roundness of them, her long hair drifting in the current. Are you sure you're up to it?

She looked back at Jonathan. I'm fine, thank you.

Did he do that too?

What?

Your back.

Oh those. Yeah. My scars of honor.

Scars of honor?

Every time I'd run, and he'd catch me, I'd get a fresh new set.

I'm sorry.

That's all right. He can't do it again, can he?

No.

Thanks to you.

I'm just glad you're okay.

Are you?

Yes.

So what'ya say, can ya swim?

You have the longest hair I have ever seen.

You like it?

Yeah.

I haven't cut it since I was a little girl.

It's nice. I like it.

You said that.

He cupped his hand and splashed her face. I know I did, and he dove under the water.

She waited for him to surface. She turned and looked in the direction of the shoreline and waited for him to surface there, but he didn't, breaking from the water at the mouth of the river. Coming?

She smiled and dove under the water.

He waited for her, and together they swam out into the big water of the lake, two distant forms of body and will alone in their being together in the vast quietness of this place.

They stopped swimming and began to tread water.

It's beautiful, isn't it?

Jonathan looked too. It is.

Oh my god.

Jonathan looked to where Holly was looking, at a big bull moose, swimming toward the shoreline.

Too bad we didn't have a rope, he said, we could hitch a ride back.

No, thank you.

It'd be all right, you just need to know when to cut the rope and let go.

You know what?

What?

I could live right there, and she pointed to the top of a high cliff that ran up from the water. I'd build a house.

You'd have a nice view.

Yes, and no one around for miles.

You might get bored up there, all on your own.

Oh, I don't know. She looked at Jonathan. I could have visitors, from time-to-time, I suppose.

Holly's a nice name.

Thank you.

He looked back to the river shoreline where their clothes were. We should start back.

All right.

If you get tired, just let me know, and we'll stop and rest.

They started to swim, side-by-side.

They reached halfway and Holly stopped.

You okay?

I need to rest for a minute.

That's all right. He watched her struggle to tread water, and he moved closer and turned his back to her. Wrap your arms around my neck.

No, I'll pull you under.

It's not far.

Yes, it is. You won't make it.

I'll be fine. We need to keep swimming.

She wrapped her arms around his neck and the weight of her pulled him down. He lifted his chin to keep his mouth above the water.

He looked back. You kick too.

He moved his arms out under the water and drew them back again, and they both kicked. He did it again, long, hard strokes, both of them kicking and moving through the water, the skin of their bodies pressed to one another, the good feel of the lines of her body, the smoothness of her skin, her breasts, the fullness of them pressed to his back, her hip bones, her pubic crest bone pressed to his lower back. And they swam like this, as if one, some watery conjoined thing moving slow and easy and through the stillness of the water.

Jonathan touched bottom and Holly let go and swam until she touched. He placed his hands behind his head and stretched out his back.

I'm sorry.

That's all right, it wasn't far.

It was far enough.

I'm fine.

You have to turn around.

He turned around, and she walked from the river, her thin, curving body dripping water, her long hair hanging wet down her back. She looked over her shoulder at Jonathan, and she stepped from the river. She rubbed the water from her with both hands and picked up her panties from the bush and pulled them on by the two thin straps that ran across her hips. She pulled her dress over her head. You can turn around.

He turned around and watched her lean forward and wring her hair out. She flipped it back. Ya comin out, or not?

He waited for her to turn around.

She didn't, and she looked at his jeans hanging over the bush.

Holly, no.

She picked them up and stepped into the river and held them above the water. C'mon, cowboy, out you get, or in they go.

Funny.

Who's kidding?

He stepped forward until the water was at his waist. Holly, don't, they're the only ones I have.

Oh?

He stepped forward again and stopped.

Chicken, and she threw his jeans back onto the bush and ran up the pathway. I'll meet you at the car.

He watched her run, waiting until she disappeared behind the rocks and trees before stepping out from the water.

At the top of the hill, she stopped and looked at Jonathan, walking from the river. She smiled, and turned away, and she walked toward the car.

He opened the car door and shut it behind him.

You must be exhausted, Holly said. Especially after driving most of last night.

A little. Any idea where we are?

Not really.

Was he your dad?

Rooke? Fuck no. My dad was a good man. He was a kind man, and he worked hard every day. She looked at Jonathan. The two of them were worlds apart. Rooke was my guardian, if you want to call it that? More like my jailor and pimp.

Guardian?

After my parents died, my aunt was the only family I had. They weren't married or anything.

What happened to your parents?

They died in a car accident when I was twelve. By the time I was fourteen, my aunt had left and it was just Rooke and me. He was okay at first, but then he stopped going to work at the store and started to hang out with a bunch of assholes. I moved out to the trailer to get away from em. But it didn't work. She turned in the seat and leaned against the door facing Jonathan. She brought her feet up onto the seat and hugged her knees. The first time it happened, it was just some drunk friend of his. He broke into the trailer in the middle of the night and raped me.

I'm sorry.

Rooke caught em, and actually beat the shit out of em. But after that, that's when it started. I tried to run away, but he'd catch me and bring me back. Eventually, he put a board up over the window and locked the door from the outside. But I'd still get away. Anytime one of his stupid drunk friends passed out, I'd run. But it never worked. He always got me. But I didn't care, I told myself, I'd rather keep trying and take another one of his shitty beatings than not try. She looked out the windshield, at the road waiting there for them. After that he just went ahead and put a chain on me. She slipped her boot off and showed Jonathan the red-ringed scar and heavy bruising around her ankle. She put her boot back on and looked at Jonathan. Turns out he'd been charging em ever since that first time. You have no idea how many times I've dreamt of killin him.

He's dead now.

Yes, he is, thanks to you.

I'm glad you did it.

Me too. So, where's your horse?

My horse?

I saw you on a horse.

You did?

You rode by our house early one morning. I thought for sure you were gonna see me.

Where?

Out front by the road, but it was still sort of dark. You can't see our place from the road, and my chain didn't reach all the way, but it did to a large rock close to it, and I'd sit and watch to see if anything would come by. Of course, nothin ever did. And then that morning, you rode by on your horse, and that, I had definitely never seen before. I thought about calling out to you, but I was too afraid and didn't know if that'd end up causing me more trouble than I already had. In fact, I was worried you did see me cause you stopped when my chain hit the rock.

Was it by a store?

Yeah, Morningstar's. That's us. Or was. On my daddie's side.

Was?

After my aunt left, Rooke sold it. What the hell he did with all the money that wasn't rightfully his, I'd like to know. Most likely he drank it up and gambled it away. Course I don't see how, since he made so much money off of me. But with Rooke, you never know.

The people there now seemed nice enough.

I don't know. I've never been back since my aunt left. When I was little I'd go every day after school and help my mom and dad. All day Saturdays, too, working behind the candy counter. Was it still there?

I think so. By the cash register?

I used to help my mom make it at the house on Sundays. Are you okay to drive?

Yeah, I'm fine.

Are ya sure? We could sit here longer if you wanted to?

No, that's all right, we should get going. He turned in the seat and started the car. He looked back at Holly, and smiled. I'm glad you're here.

I am too.

He put the car in drive and pulled onto the road.

They drove for a while, the sun warming them through the windshield. Holly nodding off.

He drove northwest, the direction they'd been driving the night before and soon the landscape began to change, the granite outcroppings growing larger and the woods next to the road beginning to thin, with less hardwood and more evergreens and young birch trees.

There was no one else on the road, and Jonathan drove looking beyond the road in all directions. There wasn't any sign of his dad's pickup. He looked again at Holly and the difference he saw in her face with the sun upon it, how her skin in the places not swollen and red seemed pale and smooth, and so beautiful, and he couldn't help look at the outline of her body beneath her wet white dress. Asleep in the daylight.

They approached a Parker truss bridge and before it a side road that ran north. He stopped and Holly woke.

Sorry. I was just trying to see what's up there.

I slept again. She looked out her window. There was a sign. Gabo 82. We could try up there?

Jonathan looked back at the bridge, and Holly watched a young boy walking in an open field. He had long blond hair, long past his shoulders. He was short, and there was a dog.

Looks like a wolf, said Holly.

Jonathan turned and looked too.

There was a small girl sitting in the moving grass, her back to them, her long full hair falling away. The boy walking to her. The dog out front. They watched him for a while, walking down from the northlands, easy and without thought, or so it seemed to them.

Jonathan turned right, and they drove up the side road.

The land began to roll, and to their right was a field of corn. To their left, a long narrow hayfield. Beyond the hayfield, a wide river with low banks lined with large overhanging willows and tall dead grass.

I feel like I could drive and sleep forever. Any sign of your truck?

No, nothing.

She curled up on the seat and put her head on Jonathan's lap. Would you hate me if I slept again?

No, of course not. He looked down at Holly, and he put his hand to her head. Sleep as long as you like.

He looked out his window at the river bending farther away from the road, the farm field widening. There was an old gray barn mostly fallen apart, with big black faded letters that read, Lookout Farm.

He pulled into a small gravel parking lot at a roadside diner and stopped. Across the road was a small red brick church with two wooden steeples, one at the front and one at the back.

Holly lifted her head.

I thought you might be hungry? It's the first place I've seen.

I am. I'm starving.

Jonathan got out and looked down the road. There was nothing. Everything was quiet and unmoving, and he looked back in the car at Holly, the rearview mirror tilted toward her, touching the swollen places on her face.

You all right?

She opened the glovebox and found a pair of sunglasses. These should help.

People will think I did it.

They might. She got out of the car and closed the door and hooked her arm through his. But you didn't, so don't worry about it.

They walked into the diner.

It was empty. They walked to a booth by the front window and took a seat.

I'll be right there, said a small old woman with long gray braided hair standing behind a counter washing dishes.

What do you feel like?

I don't know, said Holly. I could eat it all, I'm that hungry. You?

I could eat a breakfast.

Sounds good.

Will ya be havin coffee?

Jonathan looked at Holly.

Regular.

He looked at the woman. Two.

I'll get your coffee and be right back to get your order.

This is nice, said Holly.

It is, isn't it, said Jonathan.

The woman brought their coffees and set them on the table. She pulled an ordering pad and a pencil from the pocket of her apron. What'ya have?

Can we get a breakfast?

Course ya can.

I'll have two eggs over, bacon and toast, please.

Same for me. Oh, and a plate of pancakes to share. Holly looked at Jonathan. Is that all right?

Yeah, sounds good.

It'll be right up. The woman left and they sipped their coffee.

Holly looked out the window and saw a young Black girl who looked twelve or thirteen walking up the road, the sun highlighting her light-yellow cotton dress.

The girl looked at the diner and smiled.

Holly waved and the girl waved back. Holly looked at Jonathan. She's pretty.

Yes, she is. She seems happy enough.

Maybe that's what makes her seem so pretty? Holly picked up her coffee and took a sip. So, and that's it, that's all you been doing, riding a horse around out here in these badlands looking for your pickup?

My father died.

Oh, I'm sorry. How'd he die?

They don't really know. All his organs started shutting down, and he went a little crazy. At times, he did. Especially at the end.

I'm sorry.

On the night of my father's wake, my mother went missing.

Missing?

He nodded and sipped his coffee.

So, you're looking for your mother and your pickup?

Yes.

Do you think she took it?

No, it wasn't running when she went missing. Only after. That same night, someone broke into our house, which is when the Colt went missing.

The waitress returned with their plates of food and placed them on the table. I'll be right back with a refill.

Wow, look at all this, said Holly.

Hope you're hungry?

I am.

The woman returned and refilled their coffees. Will there be anything else?

No, that's it. Thanks, said Jonathan.

Holly poured maple syrup over the plate of pancakes. Does it bother you?

What?

She looked at Jonathan.

He put his knife and fork down and picked up his coffee and took a sip. No.

Not even just a little?

Nope.

Why?

Because it wasn't you, it was Rooke. Do you miss them?

Who? My parents?

Yeah.

Every day. What about you? I mean your dad?

He looked out the window, at the road picking up the sun.
Yeah.

They ate the remainder of their breakfast in silence.

Holly pushed her plate away and sat back in her chair. My
God, that was good. I haven't eaten like that, in I don't know
how long.

I'm glad you liked it. It looked like you did.

What are you trying to say?

That I'm glad I didn't get my fingers in the way of those
pancakes.

Funny. So, where's this place of yours?

New Acadia.

I've heard of that.

You'd like it. Although, it's pretty quiet.

Quiet is good. I haven't had much of that.

I could take you there, and you could see for yourself.

Is that right?

If you wanted to.

Holly smiled. I'd like that.

Me too.

Hey.

Yeah.

If the kid that had your gun, is the one you're chasing, he's
not worth chasing.

He's killed five people, and my horse, and those are just the ones I know about.

That's what I mean. There's nothing good that can come from chasing a person like that—that can do those type of things. I've seen it. People like that leave no room for anything else. There's no winning with them. There's only shit-kicking and loss and more shit-kicking. And that's it.

I need to find out if he did something to my mother. I'm not afraid of him.

You should be.

He looked at Holly, and he didn't answer.

Just think about it. Please?

All right.

There's nothing good that can come from this.

C'mon. We can talk about it more in the car.

They got up and walked to the cash register, and the woman met them there. Jonathan paid and she held out his change.

That's all right, keep it.

Thank you. Have yourselves a nice day.

We will, thanks. You too.

Holly walked to the door and Jonathan followed her. He stopped and looked back at the woman. Excuse me?

The woman looked.

Did you see someone close to our age come in here today? He was probably by himself.

With a tattoo on his neck? That one?

Yeah, said Holly, that's him.

Oh, sure, it wasn't all that long before the two of you. Maybe less than an hour, somethin like that. Close to it anyway.

Thanks.

They walked out the door.

Jonathan walked around the car, looking up the road. He opened the door and got in. He looked at Holly getting in the car. Did you hear that? He's not that far. He turned the car over. We're close. He looked at the gas gauge. Shit, we need gas.

Want me to go and ask where the nearest one is?

Jonathan looked at the diner.

I'll go ask.

All right, but hurry, and he watched her walk back into the diner.

Holly called out to the waitress. There was no answer. She looked more, and she couldn't find her. She stopped and listened. Hello? She listened again. She walked to the back of the diner. She called out again, excuse me? There was still no answer. She came to a door opening covered with strings of beads. Hello? She waited and when the woman didn't answer, she started to step through the beads, and as she did, she felt a hand on her shoulder. She screamed and jumped back. She looked behind her. You scared me.

Sorry about that. I was in the little girl's room. Can I help ya?

We were wondering if there was a gas station nearby?

Oh, sure there is, just keep goin up the road. It's not that far at all. Maybe a couple of miles.

Thanks.

My pleasure.

Holly left the store and got in the car. She said there's one just up the road a couple of miles.

Jonathan looked over his shoulder and pulled the car onto the road.

They passed a side street that ran next to the little church and on past the diner. Beyond the side road on the right was another hayfield, to their left, a cemetery, and after that, more rows of field corn. He looked at the gas gauge. Can you see anything?

Not yet.

She said it wasn't far?

There it is.

It was a Texaco station, and he pulled up to the pump and stopped.

They got out, and Jonathan started to pump the gas. He looked at Holly, her head tilted back stretching her neck out, the sun on her face. She ran her fingers through her hair and into her scalp. She looked at Jonathan. I'm gonna find a washroom, I should've gone back at the diner.

He pointed to the right side of the building. It's over there.

I'll be right back.

He pumped the gas, and he looked across the road at an abandoned drive-in theater. The single screen ripped at the top right corner, rows of short metal speaker posts coming up from

166

the gravel amongst clumps of tall grass and weeds and looking very much as if congregated, and waiting for something to happen.

The pump clicked off, and he hung up the handle.

He walked to the door of the service station and opened it. He stopped and looked down at the sticky brown tiles, at a wide stream of blood.

Shit, said Holly.

Jonathan looked at Holly standing behind him at the open door. Go back to the car, he said, and he stepped inside. It was quiet, and he listened to the sound of swarming flies. He stepped forward and looked over the counter at a large middle-aged man sitting on the floor with his head leaning against the back wall, blood leaking from several holes in his chest.

Is he dead?

He walked to the door and took Holly by the arm. We gotta go.

The screen door slapped shut behind them, and a young boy, with a ragged haircut and an open bag of chips, peeked around the edge of a shelf and watched Jonathan and Holly leave. He took a chip from the bag and put it into his mouth and began to chew.

Jonathan opened the passenger car door for Holly. He walked around the back of the car and opened his door and got in. He turned the car over and put it in gear and pulled onto the road, Holly looking back at the station.

Leonard sat in an open field of fresh cut grass. Dead washed blue eyes in the sunshine.

In the distance rode two riders.

He looked, and it was unclear if he saw them.

He looked back down, his cropped hair matted with wet patches of fresh blood. Blood on his face, running smooth and heavy over his pale skin. His clothes, deep red and soaked through, pressed flat to his skin. His hands, too, fully red, as if dipped in a vast quantity of it, for he had opened her up, from her navel to her throat, the blood of her running dark over her dark skin. He titled his head, the current of elation she had given to him with him still. The recollection of her beating heart. Open and there for him. All of it, and so very wonderful. This glory of her. The openness of her pressed fully to him. The warmth of her blood, wet and thick, slipping and forming, encasing him, and his eyes, they did roll back, his own self wetting his pants.

There's really nothing quite like a fresh cut field beneath the warming of the sun, is there? A culling of an earned bounty, I suppose.

Leonard looked at the man squatting next to him, at the man's trilby hat tilted on an angle, his purple vest, green sports jacket, and red pants. He looked at the heavy lines that ran away from the man's squinting eyes. His olive skin.

The man reached into Leonard's blood-soaked shirt pocket and removed his cigarettes. He took one and tucked it behind his ear and put the pack back. Such a beautiful girl.

Leonard looked at the girl. Yes, he said softly. He looked back at the man, but he was gone.

He looked across the field, at the two men on horseback.

He looked back down at the girl before him, and he thought, what a day this is. And it was true, like the man said, it was his earned bounty. And every bit of it. And how could there ever be a better day than this one, right now? With so much bounty.

All of it earned.

By him.

He stretched back, crossing his boots, and he slept. Long and well and at peace.

They drove on and neither one spoke, Holly looking out her window at the farms they passed, with small fields giving way to long stretches of larger outcroppings of granite bedrock and forests of evergreens and scrub bush and more run-down farms, large, lone-standing oak trees.

Jonathan pulled the Impala off to the side of the road and stopped, the car idling. There's nothing but this. He nodded toward Holly's window.

I saw a side road, back by the diner.

I did too. We could try there.

Or, we could be smart, and just turn around and go.

Jonathan looked at Holly.

What are you gonna do if you find him?

He didn't answer.

Kill em? Is that your plan? Is that what you think you're gonna do?

He's out there somewhere and most likely waiting to do more of that. He looked back toward the gas station. What are we supposed to do?

Leave it alone.

How?

Make it not matter, and put it behind you. You don't know what could happen, honest to God, you don't, so why risk it?

Jonathan looked behind him. Let's check the side road, and if we don't see anything there, we'll try up ahead a bit more, just until it's dark. If we don't find him by then, we'll call it quits and head back.

Do what ya like, but I think we should go now. Nothing's black and white, Jonathan, and rarely happens as you think it will. I'll be honest with you, I'm scared, and I don't scare easy.

Not much longer, all right? He reached his hand out and put it on her arm. Just until dark, I promise.

He turned the car around, and they drove back the way they came.

And somewhere, at the edge of The Valley of Dry Bones, an old woman lit a cigarette and blew out the match. A coyote on a high ridge watching.

They turned east on the side road. On both sides were woods and shield rock. The road turned right, and coming out of a bend they climbed a hill, the road cutting through high cliffs of granite. On their left was a small farm with a run-down, red brick Victorian house. A tumbled cedar fence ran across the front yard, the lawn in need of cutting. A gray wooden garage in disrepair at the end of the driveway. An older model Massey Ferguson tractor parked on the far side of it, tall grass growing up around the wheels.

This is the first place we've seen, said Jonathan.

And there's been no sign of him anywhere. Is there any point in going any farther?

No, I suppose not.

He pulled into the driveway and backed onto the road. He put it in drive and started back down the road, Holly looking back at the house, at a young girl alone in the backyard on a rusted swing set that squeaked as she swung. She stayed looking until the girl dropped from her view.

Anything?

No, nothing. Just a little girl on a swing.

They came to the main road and Jonathan stopped. We'll go a little farther north, it'll be dark soon, and if anything, we can find a place to pull over and sleep. We'll head back in the morning.

Are you sure?

The hell with it. Maybe the people back home found my mother and that'll tell us everything we need to know. In a lot of ways, I wish I'd never left. He looked at Holly. Other than meeting you, of course.

I'd like to see the store.

That's a good idea.

You don't mind?

No, not at all. And your place. We'll have to stop there.

Oh?

In case you wanted to get some things.

Things?

I don't know, I just thought—.

It's a good idea. I forgot, you've seen my place already. So, it's fine.

Let's find a place to spend the night. At least part of it, anyway.

Holly stretched back against the door, her feet on Jonathan's lap. Cowboy?

Yeah?

Don't make it too long from now.

No, he said, and he smiled. I won't. He turned right and headed north.

PART SIX

Leonard crested a steep hill and slowed the pickup and made a hard turn right. On the left was a large valley, the sun low, highlighting the tops of tall white pine trees. He slowed more and looked at the valley. The road bent left again. Past the trees, he saw a large gorge running the full length of the far side of the valley.

He spotted a trail and pulled the pickup off the road to the right and parked beneath the covering of a large white oak tree at the edge of a field.

He turned the truck off. He was tired. The girl's blood still wet on his clothes. He got out of the pickup and crossed the road and started down the trail.

The valley was cool with pine needles covering soft loose dirt that shifted under his feet. He approached the river at a spot where it widened and bent south. He squatted at the river's edge and felt the water. It was cold, and he lifted some with hands to his mouth and took a drink, the sound of the rushing gorge loud over the valley floor.

He walked to a large rock and sat and took his boots off. He had no socks. He took his cigarettes and lighter out of his shirt pocket and placed them on the rock, and he pulled his shirt over his head and dropped it to the rock. He undid his belt buckle and stepped out of his pants and gathered up his clothes and walked to the river's edge.

He dropped his clothes and entered the river walking until the water came to his waist. He lowered himself to the base of his neck, such that it looked as if the open jaws of the dog tattooed on his neck was drinking in the river water. He lowered himself farther, to the level of his eyes, and he circled, slowly, taking in the valley beneath the fading of the day, and he thought of the woods before him, just like the ones when he was a small boy, behind their house, days spent playing his games, all alone, and staying out well after the sun had fallen and walking home in the dark and taking a beating for it.

He fixed that soon enough.

True enough.

And fixed it well.

He watched and he studied, looking for patterns, his patience well assured. And then, rewarded for it. Lesson learned well. Mechanics without thought. Trusting and accepting of what he could become. This drive to the understanding of himself. Without emotion. Total control. He'd wait and drop the mason jar over them. He smiled, thinking of it now. Young and learning, the certainty of the outcome, and how it brought him such happiness. Complete fulfillment. And still did. No fear. No self-doubt. Just this righting of himself. A gift, he thought. His alone. At least, he'd never met anyone else like him.

He hoped one day he might.

He liked to put his face to the jar, tilting his head, trying to see what he had come to understand he would never see, but still held hope he would one day. He liked knowing they were trapped, and watching their fear come, and what they might do. That moment of their realization, and then the panic.

It never failed and always there.

He'd burn their eyes out, not for the pain, that didn't matter, it meant nothing. Most times with a magnifying glass, except when the sun was too low and he'd use a stick, his grip tight on the chipmunks, without squishing them, ending the fun before it began. He'd set them down and watch them run, disoriented, a blinded path into fallen branches and dry leaves, stopping, circling, unknown and crazy-like.

Endless amusement.

And here he was now, waiting still, that same patience, only the rewards greater. Far more defined and greater yet. A road owned and defined by him.

These greater truths.

His and his alone.

He closed his eyes and tilted his head back, and he marveled at his blessings, and he submerged himself completely in the cold river water. This christening of his integrity, if not, perhaps, his eternity.

They drove back up the road and Jonathan looked west, at the setting sun, and he pushed the gas pedal down harder.

Leonard exited the water, lit a cigarette, and dropped the pack back to the rock. He smoked naked by the river, looking to the road above him.

He picked up his wet clothes he'd cleaned in the river and with just his boots on, he started up the embankment to the road.

He spread his clothes over the back edge of the pickup, and he took the nub of his cigarette from his lips and flicked it to the road.

They approached a hard turn left and Jonathan slowed through it. They came to a steep hill, and he stopped the car. To the left, a line of woods that continued along the edge of the road down the hill and back up again. To the right, a grassy field.

Should we run it?

Holly smiled.

Let's see what this thing can do, and he pressed the gas pedal to the floor, choking it out before it kicked in, the Impala running heavy and hard down the slope of the hill. By the bottom of the hill they'd hit ninety, Holly with her head out the window, her long hair streaming behind her. The car began to climb, the speed pulling back, and Holly came back inside.

They topped the hill and the road made a hard turn to the right, Jonathan having to hit the brakes hard, the car fishtailing in the loose gravel.

Holly laughed and Jonathan smiled and when the dust settled, he looked past Holly, at a large moss-covered rock pile in the corner of the field.

Holly looked too. She turned back and nodded forward. There's an area we can pull up to. Jonathan tried to see around the far bend in the road but couldn't. He moved forward and stopped and looked again. There was nothing. He turned into the clearing and parked next to a pathway that ran through a stand of tall evergreens, and he turned the car off.

Holly looked at the last of the day's sun dropping behind the tall valley pines. It'll be dark soon.

Let's have a look.

They walked the dirt path and came to an opening that looked over the valley. To their right was the wide arm of the Crowe River, flowing slow and easy, turning and running to the foreground of where they were.

Jonathan walked to a plaque mounted on a wooden post to their right. He looked back at Holly. It's called The Gut.

Holly joined him and together they looked down to where the main part of the Crowe River met with the loud rushing water of the gorge, a fissure cut into granite. Thunderous water, turning and pounding for half a mile.

It's so beautiful, said Holly.

Jonathan looked at the embankment to their left, at the rough rocky ground with large trees fallen and some caught up in their falling by other large trees still standing. Beyond the embankment he looked at the river and the shoreline that widened out and cut back toward a large overhanging cliff.

Holly looked at Jonathan. Let's spend the night here.

It'll be cold. He looked back in the direction of the car. You think he kept any blankets in the trunk?

He lived out of that thing, so possibly.

They walked to the car, and Jonathan fitted the key to the lock and opened the trunk. There were mostly dirty clothes, a scattering of tools, empty bottles. Toward the back of the truck, he found a rolled up sleeping bag, and Holly took it from him. He looked back in the trunk. Feel like a drink? He took out a bottle of bourbon with a few inches left in it.

Anything else?

Nothing really. Mostly just clothes and tools.

He built a small fire in the center of the clearing, and Holly opened up the sleeping bag and spread it on the ground next to the fire.

She sat and Jonathan joined her, and together they looked over the valley, the tops of the tall trees highlighted by the light of the coming moon.

It's nice, isn't it, said Holly.

Yes, it is.

I'm glad we're done with him, said Holly, and she leaned her head against his shoulder. And with Rooke too. She lifted her head and looked at Jonathan.

What?

No more bad things, all right. We've had enough of that.

Jonathan smiled.

Go on, do it, promise. Just peace and quiet. She took the bottle from him and tipped back a sip.

He waited until she had taken her drink, and he said, I promise, and he leaned forward and kissed her.

The moon finding them.

They looked at one another, Jonathan's hand coming to her face.

Did you promise?

Yes, I did. I promised.

What's your farm like?

What's it like?

Yeah.

I don't know. The house is old, but it's nice enough. There's a big porch that looks over the hills at the front of the house, and a wide creek with ponds, and large sugar maples and willows that line the driveway. He took a sip of the bourbon. There's a barn and a few other outer buildings and that's about it.

What'ya do there?

Mostly sheep. It's on a peninsula high up above a seaway.

It sounds nice.

It is. He took another sip and held the bottle out to Holly.

She shook her head, no, and leaned her head back against his shoulder, and they stayed like this. Quiet. Taking in one another. Taking in the night. She looked at the moon. Just for them, she thought. This is so nice, she said, and she looked back at Jonathan, and they kissed again, this falling into one another, completely, and never to be again who they were before that moment.

He was naked with his boots on and an erection. The rifle scoop to his eye. He lowered the rifle and smiled. He put the scope back to his eye.

Rachael was in the kitchen, not sleeping, restless. She'd make a cup of tea, it might help settle her, and she walked back to the study and sat in her chair and pulled her blanket over her. She wouldn't read, and she sipped her tea instead, reciting passages from Alice in her head. And it helped.

She looked at her father, asleep on the couch, and she was getting tired now, her eyes heavy, and she said, Alice.

Alice keep me.

Keep me safe and not dreaming.

Bring me to you.

Alice, please.

Jonathan was up first, standing before the valley at the edge of the lookout, the light of the morning just breaking over the trees.

Leonard opened his eyes and he sat up. He reached for his cigarettes on the dash and lit one. He opened the door and got out of the truck and slipped his boots on. He checked his clothes. He reached back into the truck and grabbed the rifle. He walked to the edge of the road and put the scope to his eye. He had a clear shot at Jonathan and he took it, the rifle shot resounding. Holly's wakening screams. Both echoing in the valley. Breaking the quiet of the still morning.

Leonard lowered the rifle.

Holly moved onto her knees and bent over Jonathan. There was blood running from a hole in his chest and from his head, where he'd hit it on a rock. She put her bloodied hands to his face. Jonathan? She looked again at the hole in his chest, and she began to shake, she began to cry. Oh God, no, please.

Leonard scoped the rifle again, his view obstructed by the low stonewall of the lookout.

He lowered the rifle and moved to his left. He put the scope back to his eye.

Holly was low on her hands and knees scrambling to the back of Jonathan. She put her hands beneath his arms and tried to pull. She couldn't move him. She pulled harder. She got to her feet and crouched over and pulled again, and she started to move him. Another bullet, ripping past her head. She dropped to the ground screaming.

Leonard lowered the rifle. He leaned it against the truck and opened the door. He reached for his cigarettes and lit one. He tossed the lighter back in the truck and closed the door. He smoked, naked with his boots on, his erection back again, the drive to it pushing him on, keeping him there, active and alive, reaching to these dreams of his unleashing. Dreams of back alleys with wet cobblestones under dim lights where fucking was only ever fucking unless it was amongst blood and pain, and he smiled. These thoughts of her. Both of them. Caught in his mason jar. Oh yes you are. And just how long could he drag this out?

Step-by-step.

Measured and assured.

He picked the rifle back up and put it to his eye, and he watched Holly dragging Jonathan away from his reference of sight. He lowered the scope and moved more to the left. He lifted the rifle again and saw Holly through an opening between the evergreen trees, crouched over Jonathan, resting, and he pulled the trigger.

The bullet entered Jonathan's leg and Holly screamed and dropped to the ground. You fuckin asshole, she screamed. Who the fuck are you? Just fuck the fuck off and leave us alone! She crouched again and pulled Jonathan harder, her fear and hatred, the refusal of hope dying, pushing her on. She was crying, and she dragged Jonathan the rest of the way to the car.

He flicked his cigarette away and lifted the scope back to his eye, watching Holly reaching up to the passenger door. He fired.

The bullet hit the door. Holly screamed and lowered her hand.

She waited, her body shaking. She reached up, her hand finding the door handle, and she pulled, another bullet ripping into the door. She screamed again and lowered her hand.

Leonard smiling. He lowered the rifle.

The door was ajar and she opened it from the bottom, and with the cover of the door, she crouched over Jonathan and tried to lift him.

Leonard sighted the door window and fired, the glass shattering. Holly dropping to the ground.

She wiped the shards of glass from her back and waited. She put her arms around Jonathan and lifted, pulling him up until his back was against the front seat. A bullet shattered the backdoor window, and Holly fell over Jonathan. She lowered herself closer to the ground and wrapped her arms around his legs and began to push him up onto the seat. She folded his legs into the car and she climbed into the space between Jonathan and the dashboard and crawled forward. She sat on the seat behind the steering wheel, staying low, her body flat to the seat next to Jonathan. She looked at his blood-soaked face, and she said, don't die.

She started the car and dropped it into reverse and without looking she backed the car up.

Leonard lowered the scope. Fuck, he said, and he started to run, the rifle in his hand, and he came out of his boots. He sprinted to the bend in the road and made it there just as Holly sat up and dropped the car into drive. He sighted the rifle and fired, the bullet taking the rear window. Holly screamed and crouched behind the steering wheel. Another bullet taking the windshield.

On the down slope of the hill, Holly stopped the car and put it in park and reached over Jonathan and closed the door. She sat back up and dropped the car into drive and hit the gas.

Leonard was walking. He came to his boots and put them on. He walked more, and soon he came upon a Jesuit priest with white hair and a long walking stick. Leonard stopped.

Morning, my son. Hunting?

Somethin like that.

Chilly?

Leonard looked down.

The need to hunt just suddenly came over you, did it?

Possibly. Have a nice day, priest.

And you, my son.

Leonard stopped and walked back to the priest. Why do you think I'm your son? I have no interest in being your son. Why would I? I had a father, and I killed him. I had a mother, too, and I killed her.

Just a figure of speech.

I have a question.

What's that?

Who shall inherit the earth? You? Those blessed by Him, and Him alone. Is that right? The way it is?

Yes.

The meek shall inherit the earth?

Yes, of course. The damaged and the broken, for they are the meek, those for whom the shell of their vanity has been cracked wide open, and thus able to receive the true glory and the light of the word that is His word. But what is that to you? Nothing, I suppose. So, fine, take these words and wrap yourself in them like an ointment and heal yourself and do something good, anything, provided it has meaning to you and can be made true by you. For what else is there?

Nothing, priest. Enjoy your walk.

And you, my—, enjoy your day. And remember this, truth in all things.

Yes, I shall. Truth in all things. He leaned forward. Truth in who I am and in what I am, is that not right? He took the priest's face into his hand and turned it toward the valley. And what of that, priest, the eyes of the unseen before us, watching us now, their will visible only to them. There and waiting, wanting, and never not there. What of that?

The priest didn't answer.

So do that, show me one place on this good earth where the meek shall inherit anything but dust and dirt? And more of it. And then, with the passing of hope dying, the same thing, just more shit, over and over. You and your false God of Hope doing nothin but keeping them there. He took his hand from the priest's face.

The priest looked at the rifle in Leonard's hand. Good day, my son, and he started to walk away.

And what of you? You and your will?

The priest kept walking.

Leonard waited. That's what I thought, and he lifted the scope of the rifle to his eye, sighting the back of the priest's head. He held it there. Bang, he said, and he smiled, and he lowered the rifle.

He opened the pickup truck door and tossed the rifle onto the backseat. He removed his cigarettes and took one from the pack. He reached for his lighter and lit his smoke. He walked to the back of the truck, slipped his boots off, and got dressed.

Her eyes were red, her face swollen and flushed. She looked in the rearview mirror. There was nothing coming. She slowed a little and looked at Jonathan, at the blood on his face and on his chest. His leg too. She checked the mirror again— still nothing. She took her foot off the gas and hit the brakes, the car in the loose gravel fishtailing and moving sideways. She put it in park and slid toward Jonathan and put her ear to his mouth. He was still breathing.

She looked out the shattered windshield, and she looked behind her. She moved back behind the steering wheel, dropped the car in gear, and turned left up the side road.

She hit the gas, looking in the rearview mirror.

She slowed through the first bend and accelerated again, the Impala unwinding and climbing through the high cuts of granite. She crested the hill and began to slow again, looking for the house with the young girl on the rusted swing set. The house came into view, and she turned into the driveway.

She turned the car off and started to leave. She stopped and reached back into the car and grabbed the Colt from the front seat and tucked it into the back of her jeans. She ran to the door and pounded on it with her fists. Hello. Anyone? She pounded harder. Please, we need help. Hello? Her right hand gripping the pistol behind her.

The door opened.

He's been shot. She moved toward the car and stopped. She reached back and placed her hand on the man's arm. Please?

The man looked at the Impala. He looked back at Holly.

I think he's dying.

Let me get my shoes.

Holly reached the car and looked back at the man following her. He looked at the gun tucked into the back of Holly's jeans. I'd feel a lot better about this if you gave me that.

Holly looked at the man, and she looked at the young girl from the swing standing at the open front door in the shadows of the hallway. She reached behind her and pulled the gun from her pants and gave it to the man.

He opened the chamber and emptied it, and he put the bullets and the gun in his pant pocket. He leaned in the car and pulled open the hole in Jonathan's blood-soaked t-shirt and looked at the wound. He leaned farther into the car and moved Jonathan forward. He looked back at Holly. It came out here.

He looked at the gash on Jonathan's head. He looked at Jonathan's blood-soaked jeans. We need to get him in the house.

Holly and the man turned Jonathan in the seat, and the man lowered himself and let Jonathan's upper body fall over his shoulder. He stood and carried him toward the house.

Rachael stepped aside, watching her father and Holly enter the house. She looked back out the door, as if to see if there were any others arriving in some form or other not yet imagined by her. She stepped into the house and closed the door.

Leonard came to the field of the slain Black girl. He slowed and pulled off to the side of the road. He put the truck in park and let it idle. He smoked, staring at the field, at the early morning light. At the blue sky running away from him, and he thought about how beautiful the day was, and how it might just get better yet.

There was a long-paneled hallway. A worn woolen runner. Framed pictures. Dark strip hardwood floors dry and creaking beneath the weight of this moment, of blood again. Blood in the house. In the morning. More death.

Death here.

Death waiting.

Leonard pulled onto the road and drove again. He came to the diner and turned into the parking lot and parked amongst the other cars and pickups and walked inside.

The people in the diner turned and looked, as if they knew, as if, within their collective consciousness, they had said, such a man as this.

He smiled. Have a good look, he thought. Bask in this glory. Soak it up.

He saw an empty table by the window and sat there. He ordered steak and eggs and fries. His coffee arrived and he took a sip, his coat still on, and he looked at the others still occasionally looking back at him. You know me. Each and every one of ya know me. You do. Now look away in your shame. He stubbed out the butt of his cigarette on the underside of the table and he looked at an old man still staring at him. What is it, old man? What do you see? You're just like me, this whole goddamn room full of men is just like me, and not something more, because you just remember this, it was said, and I'll say it, too, one man is one man and ten men is nothing more.

His food arrived and he smiled and nodded at the old man.

The overhead white globe kitchen light flickered when it was switched on. Rachael looking up at it. It'll burn out soon, she thought. She looked at the boy's long legs hanging over the edge of the wooden table.

Boil water, sweetie. Lots of it.

She looked at the blood running. Blood on the floor. Such a mess. And oh, look at his face.

Rachael?

She looked at her father.

Boil water. Use the big pot.

Holly looked at the man. He'll be all right, won't he?

I don't know, I'm not a doctor. Go down the hall and turn left. There's some whiskey in my study. Bring it here.

A scratching, screeching sound, and Holly stopped and looked back at the young girl pushing a short white stepping stool across the kitchen floor.

Holly walked back down the dark hallway.

Rachael bent over and removed a large pot from a cupboard next to the stove. She stepped onto the stool and filled the pot with water. Her father joined her, reaching over her. I'll get this. Run and get the first aid box. And bring some clean towels.

He placed the pot filled with water on the stove, and he turned the element up high.

Holly returned with a partially filled bottle of whiskey. He took it from her, and he reached into a cupboard and removed a glass. He looked at Holly. When it boils, drop these dish towels in. They won't need long.

The man ripped Jonathan's shirt open, and he opened the bottle of whiskey and poured some into the glass and took a sip and poured some from the bottle onto Jonathan's chest wound.

Rachael returned with the first aid box and several folded white towels and placed them on the table next to Jonathan. She looked at his face again, at the thick runs of bright blood.

Open it up.

She took the box from the top of the towels and placed it on the table, her little fingers struggling with the snap on the front of the box.

The man looked back at Holly. That should be fine. He pointed to a drawer next to the stove. Use something from in there.

Holly opened the drawer and removed a long wooden spoon. She fished out the dish towels and let them drip above the pot.

Rachael managed the latch and opened the box.

See those packages? Open them up, but don't take them out yet.

She ripped open one package of large square gauze and then another one.

Holly walked to the table holding the dripping towels from the wooden spoon.

He placed the back of his hand to the towels. They're a bit hot yet.

Holly looked at the man, at the aged pockmarks in the roughness of his unshaven skin. His brown and gray hair parted to the side.

Rachael?

She looked.

Bring me another bottle from my cabinet. He watched her leave and when she did he looked at Holly. Are you wanted by the law?

Holly shook her head, no.

No?

No.

He stared at Holly, at the openness of her expression, her beaten face, at her youngness, and the beauty and hope he saw there.

Rachael returned with a new bottle of whiskey and handed it to her father. She looked at Holly. What's your name?

Holly.

Put one there, said Peter.

I'm Rachael.

Holly pinched a towel off the spoon and placed it on Jonathan's chest wound.

Peter cleaned the wound and the blood around the wound, and he picked up a dry towel, and patted down the wound and held the towel there. We need to lift him. Hold this.

Holly pressed down on the towel, and the man picked up the bottle of whiskey and the glass and walked to the other side of the table. He poured more whiskey into the glass and took another sip. He put the glass down, and he lifted Jonathan from the waist up and cleaned his back wound with whiskey and a wet dish towel. He dried it, and Rachael passed him the gauze and the white medical tape, and he bandaged both holes, wrapping Jonathan's chest with gauze and the tape. He eased Jonathan down and walked around the table, finishing the whiskey in his glass. He set the glass on the table. We need to look at his head. He looked at Rachael. Bring more towels and change the water out.

She started to leave.

And my shaving things.

Rachael left, the quickness of her light steps heard on the creaky stairs.

The man poured another drink and walked to the back door. He turned and looked at Holly, and he nodded for her to follow.

They stood on the small deck.

Who did this?

Holly looked at the unkempt lawn, and beyond that, a field of tall weeds. To her left past the garage a long line of thick woods. I don't know his name.

But you know who he is?

Yes.

Why's he want you dead?

Jonathan's been looking for him.

Why?

He thinks he killed his mother.

Did he?

I don't know—I guess so, yes.

Daddie?

They both looked at Rachael, her hands pressed to the dark screen.

We'll be right in, sweetie. He waited for Rachael to leave, and he looked back at Holly.

What happened?

We were tired from driving and spent the night at the gorge.

The Gut?

Holly nodded. We woke up and he was there, on the other side of the valley with a rifle.

Did he see you leave?

She paused.

Well?

Yes.

Did he follow you?

I don't know.

You don't know?

No. But I think so.

Did he see you come here?

Holly looked back toward the kitchen.

Did he?

Not that I know of, no.

But you think he's still looking for you?

She looked past the man at the swing set. I don't know.

You don't know?

No.

You can't stay here.

Please.

None of us can.

Just until we can move him.

I won't risk it. Go back and help Rachael. I'll be there in a minute.

Holly walked inside, and the man looked at the garage, and he finished his drink.

Leonard sat in the pickup in the diner parking lot smoking. He started the truck up and pulled forward. At the road, he turned right and drove back the way he'd come.

That's it, it's all we can do. The rest is up to him. He looked at Holly. There's a bathroom upstairs, if you'd like to get cleaned up.

Daddie, we can't leave him here.

He looked at Rachael.

Not on the kitchen table.

It won't be long.

We have to take him upstairs.

He'll be fine for a while. Show Holly where the bathroom is. He looked at Holly. Do you have a bag with extra clothes?

No.

She could use—.

That's fine. They look to be the same size. You're welcome to use whatever is there. With his glass in his hand, Peter picked up the new bottle of whiskey, and he walked out the door.

Holly followed Rachael up the stairs.

The bathroom's there. I'll show you my mom's things. If you put your clothes outside the door, I'll try and get em clean for ya.

Thank you, Rachael.

Leonard pulled off to the side of the road and stepped out of the truck. He crossed the field until he came to the remains of the dead Black girl. Nothing but strands of hair, shreds of clothes, and chewed bones. He looked over the field, and he looked back at the remains of the girl. He stretched out next to her, his arms back with his hands linked together behind his head, his boots crossed. He looked at the sky, blue and wide-open, blue and his, just like love, he thought, always there and waiting.

Cover me, he said, and he closed his eyes, and he could feel all the world's love. Bring me ye weary, and they shall be at peace.

And he slept.

Holly stood under a hot shower, her arms crossed, Jonathan's blood running from her.

Rachael picked up the pile of blood-soaked clothes from outside of the door, and she stood listening. She put her ear to the door, and she heard Holly crying. She put her hand to her mouth, and she thought she might cry too. For she knew, this world could be such a hard, cruel place. Filled with such sadness and emptiness. And now she did cry too. Quietly. Like so many other days.

She walked away, down the hallway, clearing the tears from her eyes.

In his study, he worried for his daughter, just ten, beautiful Rachael. Her mother dead and in peace, and may God rest her beautiful soul. He took another drink of whiskey and tried to think of what to do.

How to tell her. Sometime soon.

And he promised himself he would, and he took another drink.

In the field, Leonard woke, and he sat up.

Can I help?

Rachael looked at Holly standing at the entrance to the study in her mother's bathrobe, her long wet hair hanging down behind her. She stepped forward and helped Rachael spread a blanket over her father, asleep on the couch. Does he always sleep there?

Most nights.

Do you mind me wearing this?

No, not at all.

What about you?

Rachael looked at Holly.

Where do you sleep?

Most nights, right there.

In the chair?

Yes. Would you like a cup of tea?

That would be nice, thank you.

You build the fire up, there's some more logs there, she pointed next to the fireplace, and I'll make the tea and then we can talk, if you'd like, it won't wake him, unless you're too tired, and then we don't have to.

To be honest, Rachael—it's Rachael, right?

It doesn't matter, we can talk later. I'll be right back.

Holly looked at the red brick fireplace, and she walked to it. There were two identical armchairs, one on either side, worn-down with matching wooden end tables and tall shaded lamps. Next to the chair on the right were stacks of books on the floor and on the table. On the other table, only one small book. She looked at the far end of the room, at the large bay window surrounded by bookshelves with a heavy wooden desk and a leather swivel chair.

She removed the fire screen and placed a log on the fire. She heard Rachael making tea, and she walked to the kitchen.

Lift his head.

Holly looked at Jonathan, and she put her hand to his face.

Ready?

She looked at Rachael.

If you lift his head, I'll put the pillow under it.

She lifted Jonathan's head and Rachael put the pillow there. Here you go, put it on him and I'll make the tea.

Holly unfolded the wool blanket Rachael had given her, and she placed it over Jonathan. She pulled a chair out and had a seat. She looked at Rachael. I couldn't find a brush?

Oh, I have one. I'll get it as soon as the tea is ready.

Thank you. Holly looked back at Jonathan, and she put her head down next to his shoulder and she placed her arm over him, and she closed her eyes.

Rachael looked back, and smiled at Holly sleeping.

Leonard was driving, the window down, and he rested his arm on the door. I got ya, though, didn't I, little farmer fuck-boy? He leaned his head out the window, refreshing his face in the cool moving air. It felt good. I'm glad you're not dead, though, our fun ending before it even really got started. Where would the joy be in that? You'll need someone to help ya with those wounds, though, won't ya? Don't bleed out on me. I'm coming.

Yes yes yes, he said, I'll be there soon, and he drove on, back up the road toward The Gut. He passed the side road that ran east and stopped, the truck idling. The brake lights came off, and he reversed the truck. He put it in gear and turned up the side road.

Rachael woke and looked at her father still sleeping. She got up and put another log on the fire. Then another one. She climbed back onto the chair, pulling the blanket over her, settling her head against the arm of the chair, and she thought of her mother, and she thought of Holly, and she was quiet, and she was sad. She got up and walked into the kitchen, Holly still there, in the chair, sleeping next to Jonathan.

Should she wake her?

Probably not, she wouldn't like that.

But, oh how'd she'd love to chat with her, right now.

I bet they're in love.

Probably they are.

And she tried to imagine that. Being in love with a boy.

It was fine in all the books she read, they were some of the best parts. But she didn't know about right here and right now. Although she'd like to. She had so many questions, she thought. I really would like to wake her. And she turned and walked back into the living room.

She climbed onto her chair and pulled the blanket over her. Don't dream, she thought, not tonight. Just sleep. She closed her eyes, and a nightmare came. A bad one. Here, and haunting, and she cried out in her sleep. Long and lonely. And she began to run.

He sat in the idling pickup on the road across from the house, the Impala visible to him. He took a last drag from his cigarette and flicked the butt out the window. Well well, he said. How fortunate. He dropped the truck into gear and drove up the road.

The kettle whistled, and Peter lifted it from the stove and poured water into two mugs. He stirred the instant coffee and took a sip from one and carried the other one to the table and placed it next to Holly.

Holly woke and lifted her head.

There's cream and sugar if you'd like some?

Yes, please. Thank you. She looked at Jonathan, and she sat up and tried to straighten her hair.

He brought the pitcher of cream and bowl of sugar to her.

Thank you for helping us, I don't know what we would have done.

Rachael's father leaned against the counter next to a bolt action shotgun and sipped his coffee.

Holly looked at the gun. She looked at the man. Where's Rachael?

Still sleeping. She's tired.

She seems like such an amazing little girl.

She is. And trust me, I'm not usually the one up making coffee. He took a sip. She's been through a lot.

I'm sorry.

We can't stay here, and yet, Jonathan can't travel.

She looked at Jonathan, and she looked back at the man. No, not yet. But hopefully—.

I want you to take Rachael somewhere safe.

Me? Where?

My wife's family. It's a couple days drive. I wish there was somewhere closer, but there's not.

Does Rachael know?

No. And I don't want her to yet. I'll tell her soon enough.

And you'll stay here with Jonathan?

Just until he's well enough to travel. You can take our car.

No. You don't know this person, we all need to leave.

He nodded at Jonathan. Like that?

Jonathan's place is only a couple of days, we could go there.

I thought you said he killed Jonathan's mother?

She didn't answer.

So then, no. Not there.

Couldn't we wait, just a bit, and leave tonight, all of us together. Please.

I don't want Rachael here any longer than necessary. I'm changing the oil in the car and doing a few other things, and it'll be ready—.

No, we have to all go. I'm not leaving him, and I can't imagine Rachael will want to leave you.

He looked at Jonathan, then back at Holly.

Please.

Fine, we'll go together. But I'm not waiting too long until we do. He picked the shotgun up and walked to the door. He stopped and looked back. I've left you the Colt there.

Holly looked at the gun on the counter.

Keep it close.

She got up and walked to the front room, Rachael asleep in her chair. She climbed the stairs and walked to the end bedroom and started to look through the woman's clothes.

An old farmer ploughed his land. He stopped his tractor and stood, his hands on the wheel, and he looked at the stain of darkened blood and the white of broken bones in the cut grass and low weeds before him. He sat and moved the tractor forward. Damn coyotes, he said, and he ploughed what was left of the girl into the cold, waiting ground.

Holly tried the woman's clothes on, and she felt her tears coming again. She stopped herself from crying, and she finished getting dressed. She looked in the mirror, and her tears came, despite herself, and she couldn't stop them.

Leonard stepped from the pickup. He stretched and walked to the edge of the road, standing amongst stunted jack pines, alder bushes, and small thin birch trees. He reached into his coat pocket and pulled out his smokes. He was one-and-done in the pack, and he took the cigarette out and crumpled the pack and tossed it to the road. He smoked, and he looked at the valley below him, the red brick house, and farther yet, a dried riverbed cutting through flat fields of dried weeds and tall dead grass, short gnarled trees, and granite rock. A parched and desperate place, he thought. But not without its charms. And he wondered, if anything good could ever come from a place like this. Possibly, he thought. Just maybe.

A coyote stepped out from the other side of the pickup and looked over the valley. It looked at Leonard, and it started to walk down the slope of the hill to the valley.

Would you look at that, he said. You don't see that every day. And he wondered if it was an omen? You go on then and see what you can do. If anything at all.

Doubt it.

But you never know.

Stranger things have happened.

In the garage, Peter was at his workbench, a partially filled bottle of whiskey with him. A glass filled with whiskey. He opened a chest-shaped wooden box. There was an older model 9mm Lugar in it. Through the dusty cracked window of the side door, he saw Rachael leave the house wearing her high black rubber boots and white nightgown. He finished the whiskey in the glass and placed the bottle and the glass in another wooden box on the shelf and tucked the gun into the waist of his pants and pulled his sweater over it.

Rachael stood at the open main door. Hi, Daddie, I brought you some breakfast.

Thanks, sweetie. Bring it up here. He closed the box on the workbench and slid it to the back of the bench next to a framed picture of his wife.

What'ya doin'?

Just getting a few things ready.

Why's their car in the garage and ours outside? She handed the plate of pancakes and utensils to her father.

He pulled the high stool out and sat at the bench. We need to go, Rachael. He started to eat his breakfast.

I thought we were going Sunday?

No, we need to go sooner than that.

Why?

It's not safe here.

What about Holly and Jonathan?

They're coming too.

They are?

I'm a little worried whoever did that to Jonathan, could still be looking for him. I'm not sure, but we need to be careful, just in case.

Does Holly know?

Yes.

I'm gonna take her breakfast now.

Okay. She's not that bad, you know.

Holly?

No, your Aunt.

Yes she is, don't lie. But Holly's nice.

Peter smiled. I'll see you inside. Oh, and while you're in there, pack some things.

Okay, I will.

And thanks for the pancakes.

You're welcome.

He watched her walk away and back into the house.

I've made some breakfast, if you'd like some?

Holly was sitting at Rachael's mother's vanity, brushing her hair. She looked back at Rachael. Good morning.

Good morning. You have such beautiful hair.

Thank you.

Can I brush it?

Of course, you can.

Would you like to have your breakfast first, I could bring it up here?

Either way, it doesn't matter to me. Will it keep?

Oh yes, it's warming in the oven.

Is it okay, that I'm wearing this? Your father said it was all right, but I didn't ask you?

Rachael looked at her mother's print summer dress on Holly. I think you look beautiful. She'd want you to wear it. Can I brush it now?

Yes please, and she handed Rachael the brush.

Rachael ran a long stroke through Holly's hair. I'd like to have hair like yours, one day.

You would?

Yes, I love it so much. When was the last time you cut it?

I don't know. Around your age, I guess. Before my parents died.

Your parents died? Rachael stopped brushing Holly's hair and leaned forward. Both?

Yes.

I'm so sorry.

Thank you.

My mom died.

I thought she might have. I'm sorry.

Rachael started to brush Holly's hair again and stopped.

Holly looked back. Are you okay?

Rachael nodded her head.

I miss mine, too. Everyday. What was she like?

My mother?

Yes.

Rachael continued brushing Holly's hair. She was beautiful. She was so kind and so nice, and on some days, on her good days, I'd stay home from school so we could be together.

That sounds wonderful.

It was.

You're lucky, Rachael, to have had her in your life. Was she sick?

Rachael didn't answer.

You don't have to talk about it, if you don't want to.

That's all right. It's nice to have someone to talk to.

If your hand gets tired, let me know, and I can finish.

It won't get tired. I like brushing your hair.

My parents died in a car crash when I was twelve.

They did? That's horrible.

Yes, it was.

Rachael stopped brushing. My dad, he— .

Holly looked back and waited. He's not doing so well?

No, not really, and he won't talk about it.

He won't?

No. And he only talked about my mom once. When she first died.

Oh?

Yes, it was the only time. She pulled the brush from Holly's hair and started again from the top. She stopped. She couldn't hold her tears back, and they came, and she fell into Holly's side, her body quivering.

That's okay, Rachael, and Holly took her into her arms. You go on and cry. It's good to cry.

And she did, crying harder, with big long gasps of air to catch her breath, like it all had finally wanted to come out. The distance. The not knowing. The never arriving. This being alone, all the time.

Rachael. I was like you. Just like you. I had no one to talk to, and I think that was the worst part, not to be able to talk about it. And I wouldn't let myself cry, either, because I had to be strong. And that only made things worse because it made me angry. Just love her, Rachael, and talk to her, and remember her in your heart, like you're doing now, all the beautiful things she was, and wanted to be, for you. She'd want that, wouldn't she?

Rachael nodded and cleared the tears from her eyes, and before she could say, yes, she saw Jonathan at the bedroom door.

Holly looked, and he fell to the floor.

PART SEVEN

I 'll take some of them smokes.

Which ones?

Leonard pointed. Right there.

The older woman with an apron on placed the smokes on the counter. You're still around, I see. You workin nearby, or somethin like that?

Somethin like that. He picked his smokes up and looked at the menu on the wall behind the woman. I'll have a special.

How do ya like your eggs?

Over easy. I'll be right back.

He stepped outside and took a smoke from the pack and lit it and snapped his lighter shut. He put the lighter and his smokes in his pocket, and he looked down the road. He looked at the small brick church and took a drag of his cigarette. He crossed the road and stood before the large wooden double doors and took another drag of his cigarette and flicked it away.

He opened the door.

The same priest from the road was inside the church, on his knees facing the front pew, his hands folded before him in prayer. In the first pew, on their knees praying facing the priest, was a young Black couple.

The priest lifted his head, and he saw the door closing. He looked around, and not seeing anyone, he lowered his head and continued praying.

And he was there now, seated behind the woman. He grabbed the woman's hair, the woman screaming, and he pulled her head back and cut her throat. He looked at the man, and he smiled. You'd best join the others, and he stabbed the knife deep into the man's neck. He turned the knife, the width of the blade ripping away the man's throat, blood spraying onto the priest's cloaks.

The priest stood and backed away.

Leonard retracted the knife from the man's throat and stepped over the front pew and put the knife to the priest's forehead.

Why?

That's not the question, priest. The question is, what shall you do?

What do you want?

What do I want? To test our theory, of course.

The priest looked at the dead couple, their blood running from them. He looked at Leonard, who reached his left hand out and brushed aside a stray strand of soft white hair fallen over the priest's forehead.

The priest continued to stare at the full reach of the derangement standing before him. Please.

Yes, that's it. Just like all the rest.

The priest started to back away, and Leonard held him.

Do you not remember? asked Leonard.

What do you want?

I told you.

Please.

Am I not still your son, Father?

The priest crossed himself, and Leonard leaned closer. Not why, priest, how. And the answer, of course, is by the very will of me. He moved his hand to the back of the priest's head and rammed it forward, such that his knife penetrated the priest's neck, coming out the other side. He removed his knife and looked down at the fallen priest. Let me know how you make out with all the meek we spoke about. The very ones you did not know, or could not see. Send my regards, and he turned and walked away.

Holly and Rachael managed to get Jonathan onto the bed. He was bleeding through his bandages, and still not awake.

Rachael left to get her father.

Holly stayed, and she put her hand to his face. You'll be okay. She leaned to him, her mouth next to his ear. Remember, you promised. Nothing bad, ever again. That's us. And she kissed him. It'll work out, you'll see. Just get better.

Leonard, finishing his breakfast, pushed aside his plate. He finished his coffee and stood and walked to the cash register and paid the woman. He walked out the door.

The pickup was the only vehicle left in the parking lot. He got in and turned the key.

It wouldn't start.

He tried again.

Jesus fucking Christ.

He tried more.

He got out and opened the hood and looked at the engine. He looked around. He walked back to the open door and slammed the door shut. He opened it, and he grabbed the rifle from the back seat, and slammed the door shut again. He looked up the road. He looked at the plowed field that edged the parking lot, and he started to walk across it, his boots sinking in the freshly turned soil.

Rachael approached her father, bent over the engine of their car. Daddie, Jonathan walked up the stairs and passed out. He's bleeding through his bandages.

Peter pulled himself out from under the hood of the car and began to wipe his hands with a rag. Bad?

Not too bad, but they're pretty wet.

Get some towels and the first aid kit, and I'll meet you up there.

Okay, I will, and she ran back into the house.

He watched her go, and he walked into the garage and pulled down the garage door, the Impala hidden away inside.

Leonard came to the place where the dead Black girl should've been and he stopped. He looked down. For I have made you as clay; and I can, and I have, taken you back to dirt again. But fear not, he said. It's noted somewhere. Marked and noted, for all of us to know. If we wanted to. And I do.

And I shall.

See ya, he said, and he walked on.

Rachael entered the room with a pile of fresh towels and the first aid box in her arms, and Holly looked back at her. He spoke.

Rachael stopped. What'd he say?

He said he was glad I was here.

Oh, Holly.

Yes, and she wiped away the tears welled in her eyes.

I think we should get him something to eat, don't you? To help him get his strength back.

That's a good idea.

Like soup. I'll heat some up. But first we have to change his bandages. Rachael stood next to the bedside table, the fresh towels and first aid box in her arms, the Colt .45 on the table preventing her from putting them down.

Holly noticed and opened the drawer and put the gun there and closed the drawer and Rachael put the towels and first aid kit down.

Peter entered, and he walked to Jonathan, standing, looking. He looked at Rachael. Boil one of the small towels and bring it back up.

Rachael left with the towel.

Peter looked at Holly. Help me get him upright, and let's get these bandages off.

Leonard came to the side road that ran east and west, the sun high in the sky. He looked up and down the dirt road and he turned right, and he walked up the road.

Rachael, let me speak with Holly for a minute.

She started to leave and stopped and looked back at Holly. I'll get that broth going.

Thank you, Rachael.

They watched her leave and Holly looked at Peter. We can't move him. Not yet.

No, but we can't stay here much longer, either. We'll see how he is tonight, but one way or another, Rachael leaves here in the morning. Agreed?

Yes, agreed. Thank you.

First thing in the morning, he said, before it's light.

Rachael was swinging, pulling hard on the chains and kicking her legs out before her. The chains at the crossbar squeaking with each pass she made. Hi, Daddie. Are we still leaving?

Yes, but not until the morning.

How's Jonathan?

He's sleeping.

I'm glad he'll be all right.

Me too.

I'm making him some soup.

That's good, if you can get it into him.

I hope so, and she leaned back and pumped her legs, getting the swing going, as high as she could, the squeak growing louder.

Inside the garage, at his work bench, Peter opened the bottle and poured another drink. He looked out the side door window at Rachael on the swing, and he watched Holly walking out the back door, down the stairs, and over to Rachael. He looked at the framed picture of his wife and he took a sip. He thought, maybe she won't have to go stay with that horrible sister of yours after all.

Holly asked Rachael, can I give you a push?

Oh yes, of course, ya can. I would love that. I have the soup on.

Thank you.

You're welcome. I'm glad he's getting better.

Holly reached out and gave the swing a push. Me too. We'll be able to move him in the morning. I'm looking forward to our little trip.

Yes, I am as well. It'll be so much fun, especially with you and Jonathan. I look forward to speaking with him, once he can.

He'll enjoy meeting you too. She gave the swing another push.

My aunt's a little funny, and not particularly that nice. My Daddie doesn't think so, either, but he's not saying so right now.

He's not?

No.

Perhaps he's just trying to be polite.

Rachael looked at the garage. Perhaps. She looked back at Holly. I'm so glad you're here— I mean, not that Jonathan got shot or anything like that, just that you came here.

Thank you, Rachael. I'm glad I met you too. She pushed the swing again. But you know what?

What?

Where we're going, to Jonathan's farm, it's not that far from here.

It's not?

At least not from what I know.

You've never been there?

Nope. She gave Rachael a big push, and she ran under the swing. She looked back at Rachael. We only met a few days ago.

You did?

Yup.

And now you're gonna live with him at his farm?

That's the plan.

Oh, that's so romantic, don't you think? Are the two of you madly in love? I bet you are?

Holly smiled. I don't know, you'll have to ask him when he wakes up.

Oh, don't you worry, I will. I wanna know everything about it. This is so much better than a book. Way better.

Holly walked around the swing and gave Rachael another push. Rachael pumped her legs and looked back at the garage.

Holly looked at the garage.

Rachael looked back at Holly and said, how'd you meet?

She gave Rachael a last big push, and she walked to the empty swing next to her and sat there. She started to push herself with her feet on the ground, back and forth, slowly. He saved my life.

He did?

Yeah, pretty much he did.

How?

It's a long story.

Oh, I hate when people say that, don't you? Please?

Well, I'll tell you what. When you're a little older, I'll tell you the whole story, all of it, okay? I promise. In the meantime, let's just say he got me out of a whole lot of trouble.

He did? Trouble? What kind of trouble?

I'll tell you all about it one day, but not today, when you're older.

Fine, said Rachael, and she smiled. I'll be older tomorrow?

Holly smiled. Older than that.

Rachael stopped pumping her legs and looked again at the garage—just gliding, the swing squeaking above her.

Holly looked at the garage, too, then back at Rachael. Is everything okay?

I saw her that night.

Who?

My mother, and she pushed off the ground and pumped her legs again, the swing squeaking.

She came out there.

217

Holly looked at the back door.

I saw her from my window. It was dark, but there was a big moon, and she was wearing her long white nightgown.

Why'd she come out here?

I don't know, she went into the garage, and Rachael pumped her legs harder. Let's not talk about it. Let's be happy. We're going on a trip tomorrow, together, and what could be better than that?

Nothing, said Holly, and she leaned back and pumped her legs, getting her swing going too.

All the way to the moon, said Rachael.

Yes, said Holly. All the way to the moon and back.

Leonard was standing in the front hallway listening. There were no sounds.

He closed the door.

He walked down the hallway. The floorboards creaking lightly. At the study, he looked in. There was no one in there. He walked into the room and looked it over. He walked to the liquor cabinet and opened the door and looked inside. He walked to the desk at the front of the room and walked around it and sat in the swivel chair. He opened the top desk drawer and looked through it, moving around pens and paper. He pulled out a paperclip and tossed it onto the desk. He closed the drawer and opened the top right drawer. He reached his hand down into the deep space at the back and pulled out four pill bottles and read the labels. He put them in his coat pocket and closed the drawer.

He walked up the stairs, the stairs creaking beneath his weight. He stopped and listened, and he took his knife from his pocket and opened it. He walked down the hallway opening each of the doors and looking inside. When he came to the backroom, he opened the door, and he saw Jonathan. He smiled, and he walked into the room and closed the door.

He sat in the chair next to the bed, and he leaned forward. Well well, little farmer fuck-boy, what a pleasant surprise, and he lowered his mouth closer to Jonathan's ear. It's me, the one ya been lookin for, and you can tell me now, if ya wanted to, why it is you're lookin for me? He sat back. What'ya dreamin of? Your mother? Or are they dreams of me? Or maybe it's that snake-girl, you remember her? He stood and walked to the window and looked to the sounds of Rachael and Holly. He stepped back and looked over his shoulder. How nice for you, a new family, all packaged up and ready to go. He looked again out the window.

He walked back and stood above Jonathan. What shall we do? Shall we talk about your mother? Would you like that? Is that what you want? I bet it is. Go on then, ask what ya want. He sat back in the chair and leaned back and crossed his feet. What's that—did I have her? Is that what ya wanna know? It's been on your mind? Well, I guess that depends, doesn't it, on what you mean by that? I won't say I didn't want her, cause I did—she looked so good and lost and ready to go. You know what I mean? I guess ya probably don't.

He got up and walked to the door. We can talk about this some more, maybe later. We'll see what happens. Besides, where would the joy be in my helping you slip away in your dreams? There doesn't seem to be any sense in that, now does there? He started to go and he stopped and looked back again. Don't sleep too long, though, little farmer fuck-boy, you might miss all the fun. He started to leave and stopped again. He looked back. What'ya think is worse? Knowing she didn't care enough about ya to stick around, or thinking I was the one that did it? I'll let ya think about that, and you can answer me later, and he walked out the door.

The squeaks of the chains were slowing, and Rachael looked at Holly. Let's go inside. You check on Jonathan, and I'll check the soup.

Leonard was at the foot of the stairs. He heard Holly and Rachael entering through the back door, and he walked out the front door, closing it quietly behind him.

Holly walked into the kitchen carrying the soup bowl and spoon. I got some into him.

You did?

Not too much, just a small bit, twice.

Did he speak?

No. He didn't really wake up much.

Well at least you got some into him. That'll help.

Yes, and now I'm going to help you, and there's no saying no.

Rachael smiled. You can warm the bread up? We're having spaghetti and it's almost done.

Leonard was in the Impala. The whiskey bottle and glass in his hands. He poured a drink. Peter next to him, his head slumped forward, blood running from his opened neck. Leonard looked at the Lugar in Peter's lap. It's a good thing I found ya after all, wouldn't ya say? Ya might have made a mess of things. He took another drink. Course, ya probably couldn't have done it, could ya? He put the bottle on the seat and reached into his coat pocket and took out one of the pill bottles. He shook it. Even though it was coming, ya still couldn't, isn't that right? I guess you figured now was the perfect time to join your beautiful wife, what with that nice young couple to take care of your little girl. Otherwise, what? Were ya just waiting for me? Either way, it's done now. He looked out the side door window. He looked back at Peter. You're welcome.

He left the car and walked to the side door window. He finished his drink, and he walked to the workbench and touched the shotgun leaning against the bench. He placed his whiskey glass on the bench and picked up the picture of Rachael's mother. He looked back at Peter. Such a beautiful woman. Were you in love? You were, weren't you? I can tell. I can see it. He put the picture down and walked back to the side door window.

Rachael was draining the spaghetti. She looked at Holly. Would you mind going out to the garage and getting my father for supper? He's working on the car.

All right. I'll be right back.

Leonard, still at the door, watched Holly leave the house and start toward the garage. He tucked himself in behind the door, and he opened his knife.

Holly opened the side door and stepped inside and Leonard took her into his arms, his hand covering her mouth, the knife to her throat.

She struggled, her eyes wild, searching the garage. She saw Peter, dead in the Impala. There's no need to struggle, it's just me, we're old friends, remember?

She tried to elbow and kick him, but his grip was too strong.

Did ya miss me? I see you have a new boyfriend? Is he awake yet? I guess not. And what a sweet little girl she is, and beautiful too, just like her dead momma.

Holly stopped struggling, her eyes straining back toward him.

There we go, we're getting somewhere. He leaned forward, the Lugar tucked into the back of his pants, his knife at her throat. So, this is how this is going to go, you're coming with me, quietly, and sleeping beauty up there and little Miss Sunshine can enjoy the rest of their days, naturally, as they unfold before them. Otherwise—well, you see what I mean?

Holly nodded.

What I want is for you to get the keys to his car from his pocket, and do not make a sound. Understand?

She nodded again.

If you think I'm kidding about those two, you couldn't be more wrong. And I'm thinking, just maybe, you're tired of being wrong in this life, no? Now, not a sound, not one, and he removed his hand from her mouth.

She didn't scream.

Good, and when he took his arm away, she pushed open the unclosed side door and ran. She screamed. Rachael run!

Jonathan opened his eyes.

Rachael, setting the kitchen table, stopped. She looked toward the garage.

Leonard reached Holly on the lawn and grabbed her hair—she screamed, and he pulled her to the ground.

She yelled again. Rachael!

He said, get the fuck up, and he pulled her to her feet, his knife at her throat.

Rachael appeared at the screen door.

Rachael no—.

He covered Holly's mouth with his hand, and he looked at Rachael. Well, hello there, little Miss Sunshine, why don't you come here? It might be nice to get to know one another. Don't ya think?

Rachael shook her head, no.

Jonathan struggled to sit up. He turned himself on the bed and placed his feet on the hardwood floor. He closed his eyes and exhaled through the pain. He opened his eyes and looked to the window. He looked at the nightstand, and with the drawer still partially opened, he saw the Colt. He took it out, checked it, and tried to stand.

Tell her to get over here.

Holly struggled and tried to scream. She kicked her leg back.

Leonard pushed the knife harder to Holly's throat. She began to bleed. He looked at Rachael. Would ya like to watch your new friend here die before your eyes? Is that what you want?

Rachael shook her head again, no.

Good, then get over here.

She began to cry, and she began to push the screen door open.

Jonathan made it to the window and leaned against the wall. He bent to his left knee, his right leg with a wide bandaged wrapped around it, stiff and out to his side. He double gripped the pistol and rested his hands on the windowsill of the open window. He bent lower and tried to sight the gun down the short barrel.

Rachael, on the porch, the screen door slamming shut behind her.

Leonard, watching Rachael, suddenly tilted his head back, as if scenting the air. As if wondering, of all the world's possibilities, this day. Of all the strange and wonderful things that could possibly happen. He smiled, and as he did, he turned Holly in his arms, Jonathan's bullet ripping into her forehead. She went limp, dead in his arms.

Rachael screamed.

PART EIGHT

He woke by the window, unprepared for being alive, Rachael there, asleep next to him, tucked into his side. He closed his eyes, and he knew he was right, for wishing he was dead.

They stood before the grave of Rachael's mother, and the new freshly turned graves of Peter and Holly.

I would have liked to have taken her home and buried her there.

Rachael was holding Jonathan's hand, and through her tears, she looked up at him.

He looked down at her. Did you want to say anything else?

She shook her head, no.

Are you sure?

I just want to go. I don't know if you can understand that, but I do. I don't want to be here. She looked back at the graves, and she said to herself, I promise, I won't ever stop talking to you. In my mind, and in my heart, just like you said.

Ready?

Rachael nodded.

They walked away, Jonathan looking back at the graves. Rachael leaning into Jonathan's leg, and she cried more, and he put his hand to her shoulder.

At the Impala, he stopped and bent over, his hands on his thighs. Are you sure there isn't anything else you'd like to bring?

She shook her head, no.

All right, then.

And she fell into Jonathan's arms, crying.

He hugged her, and they stayed like this for a while. All their worlds gone, and why? That's what he didn't know, and would think about for a very long time. But not Rachael, she was too lost in this unbearable shattering of her heart, again, and she knew, she had already learned not to wonder why. And as she hugged Jonathan harder, she heard Alice, somewhere. Alice with her, and it sounded something like this: Rachael. I'm here. Wee Rachael. Rachael the Reminder. I'll always be here.

They drove through the night covered in blankets, sheltered from the cold night air pushing in through the space where there was no windshield. Peter hadn't gotten his car running, and so it was this, all that was available to them. He wasn't going to stay there. Rachael either. And there was no reason now for him not to go home. But he didn't want to. Not now. And he didn't know if he would have, had it not been for Rachael.

Probably not.

What would've been the point?

They drove through the next day, stopping to buy gas, and eating food packaged up from Rachael's house, the little girl for most of the way sprawled out beneath blankets asleep on the big bench of the Impala. Jonathan pushing back sleep, his anger and pain, the loss of Holly, and all the others, in the dark with him, and now with new words, some not yet come, waiting to be poured into these greater vacancies yet.

The Impala was parked idling at the side of the rode and Rachael sat up, half-asleep, and she looked around.

I need to sleep, Jonathan told her.

Where are we?

We're getting closer. Are you hungry?

She nodded.

All right. I'll make a fire, and we can cook something before it gets too dark.

Together they gathered firewood from the woods that bordered the clearing and soon they had a small fire burning on the loose gravel.

Rachael opened a can of stew and passed it to Jonathan who settled it into the fire. She broke open a box of crackers.

They ate in silence with the darkness coming, Rachael looking from time-to-time at Jonathan, unsure whether or not she should speak of Holly, and her dad, and the man that did it, and what he had told her. Are you gonna sleep?

Yes. I need to. But not for too long. Just a couple of hours, okay?

Out here?

227

He looked at Rachael. No, we can go back in the car, and I can sleep there.

She looked at the outline of the car in the early night. You can take the front and I'll take the back.

All right.

Can you leave the fire burning?

Yes, of course. I'll put another log on it to keep it going. Sorry, Rachael, I should have slept in the daytime. I wasn't thinking. But just a short nap, okay? Not even an hour.

Okay.

They got into the car and got themselves settled, their blankets over them.

Did you lock the doors?

Jonathan, stretched out in the front seat, sat up and looked back at Rachael. You do know there's no windshield, right?

Yes, but it can't hurt, can it?

No, I guess not. He reached over his head and locked the driver's door. Rachael sat up and locked the passenger door.

You all right? he asked.

Yeah.

I won't sleep for long.

That's all right. Goodnight, Jonathan.

Goodnight, Rachael.

Jonathan?

Yeah? He waited, his head tilted toward the back seat.

Nothin.

Are you sure?

Yeah.

228

Rachael, what is it?

I want Holly.

He turned and looked at the cold night before them through the open windshield. I do too.

Goodnight, she said.

Goodnight, Rachael. We'll be all right, okay?

She didn't answer.

Rachael?

Do you think he'll come back?

No, I don't.

You don't?

No.

Why?

I think it was Holly he was after. He has no reason to try and come after us.

What if he does?

Jonathan sat up and looked at Rachael over the seat. I won't let anything happen to you, okay. I promise.

I'm not worried about just me.

We'll be okay. I'll wake you in an hour and let you know we're back on the road, and you can go back to sleep, if you want to.

Okay.

Goodnight, Rachael.

Goodnight, Jonathan.

But she couldn't sleep. Afraid of what new dreams might come in the dark. And so she stared at the night. The emptiness. And she thought about what might be out there.

Waiting. And she wondered, did he mean what he had said to her? And what if something did happen to Jonathan? What then? The thoughts of this keeping her awake. Frightened, she became determined to never let anything bad happen to anyone she loved ever again. How? She didn't know, but she swore she would. Alice, she whispered. Help me keep my promise. Alice? Did we leave you back at the house too? She didn't know. She hoped not. Alice, she said again. And there was no answer.

In the night, the fire had burnt down to embers, Jonathan kicking gravel and dirt onto it. He got back in the car, turned it over, and pulled onto the road, Rachael asleep in the back.

He came to the clearing before the creek where Priscilla had died—murdered, and Destiny too, butchered. He slowed the car and looked.

He pushed the gas down and kept driving.

They drove on, Rachael in the back, awake now, both of them silent.

She sat up and looked out her side window. At this new world coming. At her coming to it. Her tears falling in daylight. And she heard a voice: Love is never on the run.

No, she thought.

She wouldn't let it be, she whispered.

Not ever again.

And it's nice to know you are with me still, Alice, and not left back at the house, with all the others.

And he thought, it's here with them, like the sun breaking over the horizon before them now. All this pain. And in his mind, he promised Rachael. What? He didn't know, he was tired of promises. He thought of Holly. Not like a remembering. More. He looked next to him, where she had sat. And he was angry, and he was unsure, and he had no idea, of what he knew, or what he didn't know. Not anymore. He had no idea, and he pulled the car off to the side of the road.

Why'd we stop?

See those trees?

Yeah.

That's Holly's house back in there.

It is?

Yes.

We're gonna stop, aren't we?

He waited, still looking at the trees next to the road, the place where Holly first saw him.

Jonathan?

Yeah?

We're gonna stop, right?

Yes, of course, and they drove up the long narrow rutted driveway, and soon the low house with the boarded window came into view. Holly's small trailer. He stopped the car.

Why'd you stop here?

I want you to stay in the car.

Why?

He looked at Rachael. Rooke didn't keep the best of friends.

Rooke?

He leaned forward and removed the Colt .45 from the glove box. Her former guardian. He closed the glove box and sat back.

No.

He looked back at Rachael. No?

No, I'm not staying here. She set her jaw firm, her arms folded over her chest, her eyes meeting his. I'm not staying here on my own, and if you try to make me, I'll come after you.

He looked at the house. He looked back at Rachael. Is this the way it's going to be?

She didn't speak, just staring at him still.

All right, then, c'mon. But stick close.

They approached the house and stopped. Jonathan looking at Holly's chain still pegged to the post in the dirt lawn.

The trailer door was open, swinging slowly back and forth.

Through the one good window, they could see inside the house. It had been ransacked, most of the furniture gone.

She lived here?

Jonathan nodded toward the small trailer. There.

She pointed. There?

Yes. He looked at Rachael. Come on. He held his hand out and she took it.

They must have had a dog?

Jonathan looked too. That wasn't for a dog.

They continued looking at the post and chain as they walked toward the trailer.

Rachael stopped, and Jonathan did too.

What do you mean?

C'mon, Rachael, there's something of Holly's I wanna try to find.

No.

He looked down at Rachael.

Tell me.

For Holly.

She didn't say anything else, and more tears came.

They stood looking at the little trailer. Jonathan turned and looked at Rachael. Are you sure you want to come in?

Rachael looked back at the chain and she didn't answer.

Rachael?

She looked at Jonathan. It's so sad. All of it.

I know it is. Do you want to wait out here?

No.

They stepped into the small space and stopped. Holly's things were scattered everywhere. Piles of clothes on the unmade bed, pots and pans and plastic plates and cups spread over the counter and on the floor. Flies buzzing above the unwashed dishes in the sink. Jonathan looked at the boarded-up window and the smeared words, life is good, written in red lipstick.

She wrote that?

He looked at Rachael. I don't know, but I guess so.

Rachael put her hand to her mouth. She moved closer to Jonathan and put her head to his side. It all just makes me want to cry more, and it feels like I'll never stop.

He put his hand to Rachael's head. She said she had a necklace that belonged to her mother. I want to try and find it, but I can take you back outside, if you like?

No, I want to help.

Together they began to look for the necklace, and at the far edge of the bed against the wall beneath some clothes, Rachael found the corner of a jewelry box. She picked it up and looked inside. There was nothing in it.

Can I see it?

She handed it to Jonathan, and he looked it over. He gave it a shake and there was a small rattle. He looked at Rachael, and he shook it again. He tried to pry the top off, but it wouldn't come. He held it to his ear and shook it again. He tried the top again. He wrapped his hand around the dancing figurine mounted on the top and snapped it off. There was a hole, and he tipped the box upside down and shook it until a silver chain fell into his open hand. He held it out to Rachael.

That's beautiful.

Go on, take it.

Rachael took it in her hand and ran her fingers over it. She held it back out to Jonathan.

I want you to have it.

Me?

Yes.

She smiled through her tears and together they left the trailer.

They walked back across the lawn and at the front of the house Jonathan stopped. You think we should look inside?

Rachael shook her head. I don't want to. It's too sad, and I don't think she would want us to.

He looked down at Rachael and he held out his hand. She took it, and they started to walk again. Rachael stopped and looked at Jonathan. Bend down.

What?

Bend down.

Why?

Just do it, Jonathan.

He bent down and Rachael reached up and placed the necklace over his head. This was meant for you, not me.

And now tears came to his eyes, and Rachael wrapped her arms around his neck, and she squeezed him as hard as she could, and she whispered, we'll be all right, remember?

Yes, he said, I remember, and he cleared the tears from his eyes.

They drove again, Rachael in the front seat next to Jonathan, neither of them talking, just thinking of Holly, and what they had seen, and her not being there with them now.

Rachael looked at Jonathan. You tried to save her.

He looked at Rachael.

And if you hadn't, he would have her now, and her life would have been even worse than what it was like back there.

Jonathan reached his arm out, and Rachael slid over and tucked herself in next to him.

It's true, she said.

I guess it's all true, Rachael, all of it, and it'll be with us forever. He looked out his side window, and he thought, where do I start now? How do I take myself back from here? He looked at Rachael. Good things can happen, too, right? We'll just have to see to it, won't we?

There was a large bang, like a gunshot.

Rachael screamed.

The car shook.

Jonathan looked in the rearview mirror and by the shake of the car he knew they had blown a tire. It's okay, it's just a tire.

He pulled off the road and turned the car off. He got out and walked to the back of the car and Rachael followed. He bent down and looked at the tire. We picked up a nail.

Rachael looked around, uneasy being in such a wide-open space, especially now. Is there a spare one?

I don't know. He walked to the open door and leaned in and took the keys from the ignition. He walked back to the trunk and opened it. He moved aside his dad's .303 and the scattering of clothes and tools, and he opened the carpeted covering of the spare tire space. We're in luck.

I need to go to the bathroom.

Jonathan pulled his head out from the trunk and looked around. All right, go over there. He pointed to the woods just beyond the side of the road.

Rachael looked around again. I don't know, maybe I can hold it.

He looked at Rachael. Want me to come with you?

No, she said to Jonathan. I do not.

Okay, well, it'll be all right, I'll keep an eye out.

Okay, she said, and she walked back to the car and grabbed some tissues and Jonathan watched her walk down the embankment toward the woods. She reached the woods and kept walking.

That's far enough.

She stopped and looked back. Turn around.

Don't be too long, and he looked back in the trunk. He lifted the tire from the cavity it rested in, and beneath it was a jack, a tire iron, and a wrinkled grease-stained paper bag. He leaned the tire against the back bumper and looked back in the trunk. He checked on Rachael, and he took the bag from the trunk. He opened it and looked inside. It was filled with cash, all hundreds. Jesus Christ, he said. Holly's money from the sale of her parent's store. It had to be.

He wrapped the money back up, and he looked at Rachael walking out of the woods. He put the bag back in the trunk, and he took the jack and tire iron out.

Do you need a hand?

I'm all right. It won't take too long.

Do you have horses?

He looked at Rachael. Of course, we do, a couple of them.

I've never been on a horse.

We can fix that.

We can?

Of course we can. One can be yours and one'll be mine. How's that?

Really?

Yup.

Do you have cows?

We have one cow and a lot of sheep.

Can I milk it?

A sheep?

Rachael smiled. The cow.

Of course, you can. Every morning before school, if you like.

School?

What'd you think? I was going to teach you?

I hope not.

Me too, and Jonathan smiled. Ok, let me finish this up, and we'll be on our way.

They came to the Morningstar General Store, and Jonathan stopped the car.

Are we going in?

That was Holly's, when she was young, before her parents died.

It was?

Yup.

It looks nice.

It is. I was in there when I first left. He looked at Rachael. Do you want to go in?

I don't know, I think I'm all right. But if you do—.

No, I'm all right too.

I just don't want to get sad anymore, and it'll make me cry again.

All right, we'll get going. The farm's not too far from here, and we could come another time.

We could?

Of course. We can come lots of times.

That'd be nice.

Yes, it would, I think so too. Maybe on Sundays for breakfast. We could make a habit of it.

For Holly.

She'd like that. We could have pancakes.

Oh, I love pancakes. Do you think she'll know?

Know?

That we're doing it.

He looked back at the store. Yes, I think she will.

I think she will too.

You do?

Yup. The very same way my mom and dad know I'm all right now.

Good, he said. I'm glad about that. Let's go, and he pulled the car back onto the road.

They came to the crossroad and Jonathan stopped the car. He waited, and he moved the car through the intersection, looking at the spot where he had camped that first night.

They drove on.

Is that it?

Yup, that's it.

Rachael looked at the large granite stone to the left of the driveway, the carved and black painted letters, long ago faded and chipped away. Urram Hill.

Is that the name of it?

Yes.

What's it mean?

Dignity Hill.

Why's it called that?

I'll tell you all about it another time, all right? Let's go up, and I'll show you around.

She nodded.

He looked at Rachael. Ready?

Yup, she said, ready. What about you?

Yes, he said, I think so, and they drove up the long driveway home.

PART NINE

They stood before the McLean cemetery, their horses tacked up and grazing in the field behind them.

There's so many, said Rachael.

We've been here a long time. And Jonathan turned and saw Angus walking through a gate that had been cut into the low stone wall next to the road.

Rachael looked, too, at the short stocky older man in work clothes and heavy field boots.

Did you do that, asked Jonathan?

Angus looked back at the gate. I did, aye. I'm getting too old to be climbing over that damn wall every day. And who is this?

This is Rachael, said Jonathan. Rachael this is my Uncle Angus. My mom's brother. He lives across the road.

Angus put his hand out. Nice to meet you, Rachael.

She took his wide rough hand in hers. Nice to meet you.

He looked at Jonathan. We didn't find her.

Jonathan looked at his mother's grave next to his father's.

Rachael looked up at Jonathan, unsure if he was able to take more news like that. She wanted to speak. But she was unsure what to say. She moved closer to him.

Jonathan looked at Angus. Thanks for watching the place.

It wasn't a problem at all, you know that.

We were on our way to see you, we just needed some time.

Come when you're ready. He looked at Rachael. And I imagine we'll be seeing more of you as well?

Jonathan looked at Rachael and nodded toward Angus.

Yes, she said.

Good, said Angus. I'm glad to hear it. He put his hand to Jonathan's shoulder. Welcome home. He looked down at Rachael. And you too.

And together Jonathan and Rachael watched Angus walk away, open the gate, and walk through it.

PART TEN

Holly fell from Leonard's arms.

Jonathan blacked out.

Rachael was crying.

Leonard looked to the bedroom window. He looked back at Rachael. That was unfortunate, wouldn't you say?

She didn't answer.

He walked toward her. Did you know your father was dying?

Rachael stepped back.

Did you know it?

She put her hands up before her, as if to stop him. Stop his words.

He looked back at Holly. They'd of made a nice couple, don't ya think?

Rachael looked at Holly. At the blood-soaked grass.

And good new parents for you. It's a shame, really, isn't? He leaned against the small back porch railing and took his smokes out and lit one. He won't want to live here, ya know that, right? He exhaled and shut his lighter. He'll wanna go back to his precious little farm. He looked around. I might though. I like it here. He looked back at Rachael. That'd be fair, wouldn't it?

She didn't answer. She looked at the garage.

Leonard looked too. Yup, he's in there.

She couldn't help herself, and she began to shake, and she put her hands to her mouth, and she began to cry harder.

Well, you think about it, and he pushed off from the railing, pinching off the heater of his cigarette, putting the last of it back in his shirt pocket. In the meantime, I've got some things to do. He looked back at Rachael. Just don't be too long deciding.

She watched him walk toward the woods. Did you kill her?

He stopped and looked back. Who? He looked up at the bedroom window. Little farmer- boy's mother? He looked back at Rachael. I didn't need to. She was one of the brave ones. Just like your own mother, isn't that right?

She didn't answer.

But not your father. He needed some help. And fortunately, there I was, and able to give it to him. And so it seems to have all worked out, just right, wouldn't you say? He saw Rachael look at Holly. He looked too. Well, yeah, there is that, but that wasn't my doing, was it? You can thank little farmer-boy for that one. Good luck, Rachael, and he turned and started to walk away. He stopped and looked back. Say hi to Alice for me. He smiled, turned away again, and walked into the woods.

ACKNOWLEDGMENT

All italicized words found in this book
are the words of Lewis Carroll.

SPECIAL THANKS

Kaaren Kitchell and Serena Hudson

Made in the USA
Middletown, DE
17 July 2022

69179912R00156